HELMET HEAD

Mike Baron

WordFire Press
Colorado Springs, Colorado

HELMET HEAD
Copyright © Mike Baron, 2012.

ISBN: 978-1-61475-146-5

Cover by Joe Arnold

Book Design by RuneWright, LLC
www.RuneWright.com

Published by
WordFire Press, an imprint of
WordFire, Inc.
PO Box 1840
Monument, CO 80132

Kevin J. Anderson & Rebecca Moesta Publishers

WordFire Press Trade Paperback Edition 2014
Printed in the USA
www.wordfire.com

:DEDICATION

To my wife, Ann Baron

CHAPTER 1
PROBABLE CAUSE

L arry "Red Rocket" Rodell was four hours out of Elgin with two ounces of meth in his ditty bag and one-and-a-half grams in his blood when he topped a gentle rise in Southern Illinois, saw the lushly wooded hillsides undulating into the distance and thought, *Fuck me, I'd better get off this bike, drain my lizard and do a bump if I'm going to make the roadhouse tonight.*

He felt the heat from his 113 inch S&S motor in his thighs. He felt every jolt in the old cracked asphalt from his hardtail frame. He was inured to the shriek of the bike and the roar of the wind, but Larry wasn't getting any younger. At 39 he was a full-time outlaw. He could always get a job sober and would always lose it when he showed up drunk or stoned.

Well fuck that shit. Larry was a Road Dog and the Dogs took care of their own. You could make a decent living as an outlaw. As Dylan said, you had to be honest to live outside the law. The ounces were for the club. Wild Bill promised Larry that there would be five keys coming in tonight or tomorrow, most of which Larry would take back to the Greater Chicagoland Area for distribution. Such was the economics of drugs that flowed up and down the Mississippi like the water itself. You could shoot it, you could snort it, you could stick it up your ass. And you could sell it. Larry thought meth should replace the dollar. The country would be better off on the Meth Standard. Meth was something Americans produced with pride.

Meth was the lifeblood of American labor. Assembly line workers in Beloit and Elgin lived off that shit. It carried them through the week and then it carried them through the weekend. Coke was for faggots and pussies.

Not paying attention, Larry took a gully-whumper that cracked a shock up his spine and rattled his skull. Whoa dude! Time to get off the hawg! He zipped through a hollow where the trees came right up to the side of the road. The air smelled of honeysuckle and just a tinge of pig shit, which put Larry in a nostalgic mood. He motored up a gentle hill to a plateau and there was a turnoff leading into a cornfield, two sturdy gate posts with the barbed wire pulled aside. It would have to do. He squeezed on Marilyn's brakes and the big bike slowed, front disc shrieking like a bitch in heat. He rolled Marilyn carefully off the scabbed asphalt onto the hard-packed earth, reached behind for a coffee can lid which he tossed in the dirt. He wanged out the kickstand and let Marilyn lean.

As always, he touched his fingers to his lips, then to Marilyn's, painted on the tank.

Larry semaphored his long right leg off the bike and stretched backwards, squinting into the afternoon sun. He was six four, weighed 170 with a narrow skull and the parchment skin of a heavy smoker and tweaker. His arms were so inked they were blue. His long brown ponytail fell back from his black skull bandanna. He wore Gargoyle shades. He wore a filthy gray T-shirt, now in its fourth day and over that a black leather vest bearing the Road Dogs' colors, a snarling pit bull. Over the pit bull it read in Gothic script "Road Dogs." Beneath it said, "It Ain't the Size."

The front of the black leather vest was covered with patches including "1%," "Floyd Davis/1952 - 1974/RIP Brother," POW/MIA, "Don't tread on me," and the red thirteen patch honoring Larry for giving cunnilingus to a menstruating woman.

Larry's heart went *boom boom boom*. He looked around. It was a beautiful sunny day in Southern Illinois, not too hot, not a cloud in the sky, birds chirping, the fragrance of summer on the breeze. Larry didn't see all that. Pollen made his eyes itch. He walked among the waist-high corn, unzipped his pants and pissed like a horse on a flat rock. His head felt like a cement mixer. He'd been taking a pounding all day. All his life. His back felt tight as a hurricane fence and his fingers were numb. He flexed them and swung his arms trying to bring some sensation back.

Temples throbbing, Larry returned to his hawg and removed a much-creased state map from one of the leather side bags. The Dogs were waiting at the Kongo Klub a couple miles outside Ptolemy. He'd made the run but this was a new route. The map looked like somebody threw a plate of spaghetti on the ground; there were so many winding, intertwining back roads. Where the fuck was he? Larry hadn't looked at a road sign in an hour but he had to be close. He could feel it.

He reached in his vest and removed a folded paper bindle filled with white powder. He looked around. Not much in the way of furnishings, so he shook it out right on his gas tank and used a stolen credit card to line up the bump. Not on Marilyn's face, of course. He fished a crushed plastic drinking straw from another vest pocket, bent down and hoovered.

Just like plugging in a cell phone. All his bars lit up! Yeah, baby! From Zero to Hero in five seconds flat. That bump would carry him all the way to the Kongo Klub where he couldn't wait for his first glass of Jack.

Larry straightened up feeling righteous. He glanced down the road—more loop the loops through the endless wooded hills. He looked up. The sky had changed color.

Someone had leeched the blue and turned it a sickly milky white. A tiny black dart headed east far overhead. Larry scanned his surroundings. The hills surfed into the distance like a coarse green blanket. He didn't notice the flies buzzing around his face. The tip of a red silo stuck up over the trees in a valley to the east. His eyes swept past four o'clock and doubled back.

What the *fuck*?!

Less than a quarter mile away to the northwest lay another gently rounded promontory peeking over the cornrows and this one was a county park, if you could call a patch of gravel, a trash

barrel and a picnic table a park. A county mountie straddled his Milwaukee iron and stared at Larry through a pair of binoculars.

They both froze, each instinctively recognizing his mortal enemy. Larry's imagination clicked into overdrive. How much was he carrying? Enough to bust him for dealing? Did that fucking cop have probable cause? *Fuck* probable Cause! Larry knew cops. They didn't need no stinkin' probable cause. They'd been hassling him all his life. And that cop probably knew this county like the back of his hand, and was going to be on Larry's blue ass like white on rice.

CHAPTER 2
WHITE NOISE

Pete Fagan poked through the gray bones of the chicken shack with a stick he'd picked up in the yard. Place stank of cat urine and some acrid chemical that dug into the sinuses like glass splinters. Empty plastic liter bottles littered the ground and there were three inches of scorched copper tubing. The shack hadn't been a meth lab in a long time but it wasn't a wasted trip. Every bit of knowledge helped Fagan do his job.

Kids had decorated the interior of the shack with cans of spray paint—the usual crude comments, wannabe gang symbols and a crude figure of a man drawn all in black with an oversized head waving a sword. There was a filthy mattress in one corner and scores of used condoms. Cigarette butts and empty bottles of peppermint schnapps. The place was open to the elements and various animal droppings lay on the wooden floor among the rubble.

Fagan stepped out of the chicken shack into the overgrown yard. A hundred feet away sagged the falling-down farmhouse, another casualty in the decades-long war against the family farm. Times were tough in Little Egypt. Fagan understood why some might turn to meth but he had no sympathy for them.

The grass and weeds were up to his knees. Kids had busted all the windows and painted graffiti on the side of the house. Upside-down crucifixes. Blue Öyster Cult. The Grim Reaper. A swastika. Weird symbols, random letters copied from photographs in *Juxtapoz* or *Vibe* or from boxcars that passed nearby. Teen tough guys high on paint thinner and glue. He went up the sagging steps and looked in through the missing front door. Absolute rubble. Mice and rats scurried inside the walls. The place was in receivership to a failing bank. It ought to be declared a hazard and surrounded with police warning tape, not that it would do any good.

The recession hit farm country hard. The last couple of years had been particularly difficult for the nation's solar plexus, which had absorbed blow after blow, both manmade and natural. Tornadoes swept the area in April killing four people in Bullard County and devastating a trailer park.

Why did the tornadoes always strike trailer parks? Was there something there that attracted extreme weather? The house smelled rotten. Piss and shit. Fagan turned away. The porch and yard were filled with empty beer cans and bottles. Fagan sighed and scratched his head with gloved hands. The helmet made his scalp itch.

It did give Fagan an idea, something to pursue someday when he was no longer a cop. A pig, an oinker, a jack-booted thug. He'd been called those things and worse but down here in the alfalfa fields far from the city, not so much. Rural folk respected the police unless they were running a still or a meth lab. Even then they'd smile and call you sir as they lied to your face.

Fagan's idea was simple. A motorcycle helmet lined with stiff bristles like a hairbrush so that when you moved it side to side the bristles stimulated the scalp.

His radio squawked. Down here in the valley, the reception was for shit. He'd have to get on top of one of these hills to communicate with the sheriff's office in Ptolemy. Fortunately, Fagan knew of a roadside park two miles down the road. He snapped a few photos of the graffiti with his cell phone to add to the department collection, not that they were tracking Los Zetas.

Some pot farming, a couple meth labs and domestic violence were as bad as it got in Bullard County. Occasionally they had to scrape up the pieces when some kid put his car into a tree at ninety mph, but what rural community didn't have that problem?

Of course, Fagan wouldn't have the job if his predecessor hadn't lost control of his bike during a high-speed pursuit and planted himself in the side of a barn.

They never found the perp.

Fullerton thought it was a probably a drug runner.

And the Road Dogs, a fifth rate pack of losers who dealt meth up and down the Mississippi and liked to hang at the Kongo Klub. Fagan hadn't met them yet. He planned to introduce himself the next time they were in town.

He crossed the yard, long grass swishing against his calf-high highway boots. His ride was a modified, fat-fendered, black and white Harley sporting a light bar and a whip antenna. He tried the handset but all he got was white noise. Fagan picked his helmet up off the seat. It was white with the blue and gold star of the Bullard County Sheriff's Department. He strapped it on. His scalp itched.

Fagan got on the bike, thumbed the starter and crunched down the gravel driveway to the county road. He turned right and accelerated up the hollow, the police bike as quiet as a bike can be.

When he emerged into the open, the sky looked funny. Dark cumulus were bunching up in the west and he could feel the languid touch of change on his cheek, smell it in the wind. Rain coming, maybe severe weather. There'd been no warning in the morning. Five minutes later he pulled into the county wayside, a gravel lot, a trash barrel, a picnic table and a trail leading into the woods. He kicked out the stand and spoke into the handset pinned to his shoulder.

"This is Fagan. What's up?"

Snap crackle pop. Irma Conklin, the department's veteran dispatcher answered. "Pete, Ellis Johnson just dropped in and said looks like the Road Dogs are back at the Kongo Klub. You said you wanted to be notified."

"Thanks, Irma. Where's the Sheriff?"

"Sheriff Fullerton is transporting a prisoner to Paducah."

"What's up with this weather?"

"It does look a mite stormy but we haven't heard any warnings or sirens. I'll let you know if we do."

"Thanks Irma. I'm off to the Kongo Klub."

A faint rumble off to the west drew his attention. A bolt of lightning arced from cloud to earth in brilliant dazzle. It could have been ten miles away; it could have been a hundred. Fagan waited for the rumble. One, one thousand. Two, one thousand …

The rumble came on ten. The storm was a long way off. A breeze picked up out of nowhere and rattled the alder and oak. Fagan keyed the starter, eyes automatically sweeping the horizon.

And there he was, biker at ten o'clock, peaking up over the rim of Gardner's cornfield. Fagan pegged him instantly from the silhouette—the gaunt frame, doo-wop rag on his head and the sunglasses. He could just make out the top of the dude's ape-hangers. Fagan reached into the tank bag for his fold-up binocs.

As he was bringing them to his face the biker reacted in comically exaggerated fashion, his whole body doing a snake-whip as he went rigid, jumped up, jumped down, and started the motor.

The thunderclap reached Fagan almost instantly.

CHAPTER 3
A SOUND IN THE FOREST

Fuck!" Larry spat spraying dirt all over the cornstalks and nearly sliding sideways as he torqued his hawg back to the road. He knew that oinker was coming. Larry had an outstanding warrant in Illinois. If they caught him with that much dope—it was only a couple ounces!—they'd put him away for a long time.

The sheer unfairness of the situation made him furious. He'd love to set a trap, wait for that fucking mountie to ride by and pop him with the .44 he carried within easy reach in the saddlebag. All he had to do was lean back and pull it out. He'd taught himself to fire over his shoulder like Annie Oakley. He couldn't hit anything but the effect was gratifying.

Well fuck that noise. With any luck Larry'd never see that cop's headlight in his rearview. Marilyn checked out at 106 ft.-lbs. of torque at 2500 rpm. Larry had hundreds of thousands of miles experience. No Deputy Dawg could keep up. Larry hit the road and opened the throttle, the twin cylinders, each the size of a soup can, emitting a primordial bellow as he dove back into the endless valleys enveloped by shade.

Larry was pretty sure that if he stayed on Brogden Road it would take him to State Highway 123, which led right to the Kongo Klub at the crossroads with 38. He'd been this way before but not in a long time. What the hell—they weren't building any new roads. Not in this neck of the woods. They could barely maintain the roads they had. Where the fuck were those highway dollars? Larry had seen better roads in Baja.

"Your lead, baby!" he screamed into the wind giving Marilyn her head. It was like channeling the spirits or playing Ouija—Larry's hands rested on the bars but they turned themselves. The road twisted like a garter snake. Larry kept his eyes on the dappled sunlight coming through the spread of branches overhead wary of deer.

The sunlight momentarily disappeared as a cloud passed overhead. Funny. It had been clear all day. Larry instinctively glanced in his Maltese cross-shaped rearview but there was nothing behind him save the road and the trees. A yellow info sign swished by and it took a second to register. A V-type intersection, Brogden went left, Norton Road to the right. Marilyn veered right. The narrow asphalt shimmied through the trees passing a couple overgrown pasture entries. A half mile on Larry came to another unmarked intersection and instinctively turned right again.

He had unwittingly veered into Milton's Hollow.

Clouds scudding in. Larry's heart pounding from the chase and the bump but he was pretty sure he'd lost that copsickle. That cop was probably at the state highway wondering where the fuck Larry went. Stupid cop had about as much chance catching Larry as Wile E. Coyote the Roadrunner.

"I'm a roadrunner baby," Larry sang in a surprising falsetto.

Ho shit but that put a boot up his ass! He hadn't outrun John Law like that in years! Damn if his heart wasn't wangin' like a bent piston. He had to get off the bike, smoke a cigarette. *Now.*

He looked for a place to pull over. Larry cruised slow, confident he'd lost the law. The road descended gently into another overgrown valley. Yet another pasture entrance, two ruts overgrown with weeds winding through second growth forest toward a crop of sorghum. It was so overgrown he almost missed it. Only saw it because he was cruising slowly, and just as he was passing a random breeze parted the branches and a ray of light fell on a gleaming red shard, catching his eye.

Larry stopped, turned into the ruts, and walked the big bike back until it was invisible from the road. The red shard looked like it came off a broken taillight. Little pieces of plastic crunched beneath his tires as he worked his way back, thirty feet off the road. He was in a clearing, twelve feet in diameter built around an odd, biscuit shaped mound. An Indian mound. Oak, alder, and locust trees formed a natural ceiling with a hole in the middle in imitation of an Indian hogan.

The local Indians were known as the Illinois, *duh*, adapted by the French from the tribal name the Inini, meaning "the people." They were a deeply spiritual people blah blah blah. A drunk Indian explained it all to Larry one night at a roadhouse outside Atlanta. Atlanta, Illinois. Bikers felt affinity for Indians. The bike was the modern equivalent of the horse and they were warriors at one with nature. Especially when they took the baffles out. What were MCs if not tribes?

Larry tossed down the lid, kicked out the stand and got off. Grabbing a bottle of water from the bags, he walked up the gentle incline and sat in the very center of the mound. He pulled a pack of American Spirits from his vest and lit it with a Bic.

Larry looked around. The mound had five stubby appendages. It took a moment for Larry to realize it was a tortoise. He inhaled deeply of the cigarette, heard his blood rushing through his head like an underground river. The area was supposed to be riddled like Swiss cheese with caves. Larry had never seen one. Of course he never went looking.

Glancing further into the forest he spotted what looked like a gravestone. He saw a glimpse of candy apple red. The Midwest was dotted with rural cemeteries, many informal, some lost. He briefly wondered if there were anything worthwhile. Larry wasn't above robbing graves. He'd made some serious jack stealing bronze burial urns from a mausoleum in Evanston. And those little metal veteran memorials—scrap dealers paid good money for those.

Larry ignored the rushing in his ears and listened to the

forest as best he could with his tinnitus. The breeze sighed through the trees. A mourning dove cooed. There was a sharp metallic snick, as of some blade flashing through straw.

A jagged shard of paranoia thrust into the tweaker's brain.

Larry's trapezoids clenched, the body dredging up a rumor from the subterranean depths of his soul. A black and twisted rumor like an unidentifiable body part.

The air whistled. Closer.

Larry turned.

His heart imploded as if crushed by a mailed fist. The air rushed out of him like a child's balloon. Part of him hovered nearby calmly observing that he was having a stroke and a panic attack. His eyes riveted on the figure before him.

The blade flashed, the beautiful horizontal light from beneath Heaven's door appeared and Larry's head toppled from his body, rolled off the mound and came to rest next to the turtle's front leg.

Larry saw the sky and then nothing.

CHAPTER 4

HOMICIDE

Fagan cut over to Brogden on Turkey Trail, was at the cornfield inside five but the biker was gone. He could only have gone south or Fagan would have seen him. The cop figured the biker for a Road Dog headed for the Kongo Klub. The Road Dogs lived up to their name in being extremely territorial. There'd been a number of biker fatalities over the years attributed to the Dogs who guarded their meth franchise zealously.

He'd studied the file. He knew what to expect. The president was Wild Bill Hedgecock. His Veep was Derek "Chainsaw" Gunderson, an Army veteran. The rest were a blur—Larry, Doc and Curtis, the latter two looking too old to cause trouble.

Fullerton said the Dogs were not cooking, only distributing. In Fagan's opinion this was nonsense.

Fagan came to the fork in the road and cut left, figuring the Dog would head for the pound via the quickest route. He'd gone a mile when out of nowhere a wind whooshed through the forest strong enough to nearly blow him over. Fagan leaned hard to the left and stopped as limbs cracked and part of a rotten locust tree smacked down in the middle of the road twenty yards away. Had Fagan not pulled over it might have hit him.

Fagan reached out for Irma but all he got was white noise. Fortunately the tree limb was small enough for him to rotate out of the way and lay it in the ditch. The wind abated but dark clouds with massive wrinkled foreheads scudded in. The conviction he'd been snookered abruptly filled him. The biker would assume that he, Fagan would assume that the biker would seek the most direct route to the KK.

The biker must have taken the right turn. Fagan was certain.

As certain he'd been that day a year ago when Chief Ashburton called him in and fired him.

Fagan, who stood five nine and weighed 170, wrestled the big Harley around in a Y-turn and headed back the way he'd come. A fat raindrop splattered against his chin. He looked up. The clouds were in motion, rearranging themselves. Midwest thunderstorms were unpredictable. They could dump an inch in fifteen minutes then peel off leaving the sun shining. No other drops struck as he rode back to the fork and took the acute turn to the left.

Now he was in the biker's head, seeing the road as only a biker can see it. Fagan watched for deer. Deer killed more bikers than booze and pills combined. Six minutes later he came to the second fork in the road and veered right. Milton's Hollow. Didn't even think about it. It just looked like the more interesting road. Bikers always took the more interesting road.

The rumble of electrical discharge filled the air, a freight train a mile away. Clouds cut out the afternoon sun. Fagan might have missed the turn-off if his headlights hadn't picked out the gleam of red plastic lying in the weeds. He pulled over, got off the bike, tried the radio.

He went over to the ditch. It was a taillight shard. He picked it up. It said Kuryakyn on the back. Made in China. Next to it was a crushed beer can with the stars and bars. Confederate Beer. Fagan had been surprised to learn that Southern Illinois was more gray than blue. They still flew the stars and bars down here and Saturday night the bars were filled with rebel yells.

He peered past the waving grass and saw the ruts leading

into the forest the faint outline of a road. A glimpse of metal thirty or forty feet into the brush.

Fagan took off his helmet and set it on the seat. He took off his gloves, stuck them under the helmet and scratched his head furiously. He unsnapped his S&W .40 and held it in both hands as he followed the ruts into the forest, trying to step on rocks and bare earth so as to proceed silently.

Leaves crackled. *I'm no Indian*, Fagan thought. It occurred to him to shout, "Sheriff's Deputy!" but there was something in the forest that demanded silence. Nor did he want to give himself away if his prey were in the area.

He didn't even know if the biker had broken the law, but like all good cops Fagan was familiar with body language and the way that dude reacted said otherwise.

Whoa. There was the dude's bike, black, rat and loud with ratty black leather saddlebags and ape hangers. The tank was the exception. Whoever had painted La Monroe knew his business. Fagan brought the pistol up to eye level and followed it into the clearing automatically running the clock before his eyes registered an anomaly and swiveled back to the odd mound in the center. At first Fagan thought the guy was just lying there, resting, maybe OD'ing. Playing possum.

"Sheriff's Deputy! Turn over and put your hands behind your head."

The black clad form did not respond. Fagan circled around to the side and saw that the body had no head. A soak of dark, moist brown sank into the earth which Fagan registered as an Indian mound.

The body had no head.

Fagan's heart redlined. Like he had a little tach on his chest like a Firebird. Easy now, he told himself forcing his shoulders to react. The biker couldn't have been dead more than a few minutes. Fagan spun in a circle. The forest stared silently.

Where was the fucking head?

Fagan circled the mound and saw the head nestled in the crook of the turtle's leg at the base amid a large moist spot. It must have rolled there. It lay staring wide-eyed at the sky. Blood lay on the ground. The vic had been killed in the past five minutes. Fagan approached and looked down. He'd seen that face a thousand times at biker rallies and in jails but it didn't ring a bell. He used his cell phone to take a picture.

Fagan fingered the hand unit pinned to his chest. Useless. He had to get to where the radio worked.

If the killer were using an edged weapon on top of the mound was the safest place to be. Fagan was up there in a heartbeat. He crouched by the body, pulled on the chain attached to the corpse's belt and tugged out an oversized Harley wallet. A Minnesota driver's license identified the rider as Lawrence Rodell, age thirty-nine, height six three, weight 195, eyes brown. The license had expired six months ago.

The wallet contained two hundred and sixty eight dollars in cash including a curled Franklin with white residue. It contained a business card from an escort service in New Orleans and a half-dozen credit cards, none belonging to Lawrence Rodell. The rumbling got closer. Fagan didn't want to ride during a thunderstorm but he was reluctant to leave the crime scene until he'd scoped everything that might be of value.

It was his investigation now. It was his fourth day on the job.

His eyes scanned the ground and saw where the grass had been mashed down by another set of boots. Fagan came off the mound and stooped to examine a boot print in a bare section of the moist, fungible earth. Holy shit. The print was thirteen inches in length. Had to be a size 16 XXW. Dude was a monster.

Fagan got up and walked slowly around the mound. Facing west, blood spray reached toward the forest at two o'clock. Whatever struck the biker had done so with enough force and focus to cleanly slice through bone and sinew in one stroke.

There were no samurai patrolling Southern Illinois as far as he knew. A stiff wind brought a sheet of rain that washed over him and was gone, leaving the breeze and the promise of more to come. Fagan used his cell phone to photograph the crime scene, several close-ups of the machine-like cut. A quick patrol of the perimeter revealed nothing. The wind picked up abruptly to announce a fresh downpour.

Fagan felt an urgent need to book.

He jogged back to his bike, strapped on the helmet and powered up. He did not want to be riding during a downpour. He'd done it and it was no fun. He eased out the clutch and motored down Milton's Hollow. It had to run into State Highway

123 or County Road 38. None of these little valley trails dead-ended. This was a farm state. They all led to market.

Driving with extreme care he went a mile down the road and eased off the throttle at 35, wary of rain-slick leaves. He glanced in his rearview.

A red headlight appeared a quarter mile back like a baleful demon eye.

CHAPTER 5
: DEMON EYE

Fagan pulled to the side of the road and kicked out the stand. His tires rested in weeds. Only the kickstand touched asphalt. He got off his bike and turned to face the oncoming biker, arms folded, Sam Browne belt, official in his white, blue and gold helmet and mirrored sunglasses. The red headlight dipped beneath the horizon as the biker descended the roller coaster road.

Sound reverberated through the tunnel of trees like thunder, only louder. Straight pipes. Dude was in violation of the noise ordinance. Fagan flicked on the light bar on the rear box. Red and blue strobed the sides and ceiling of a tunnel of rain-slick leaves. At least the rain had let up for the moment. The sound of the unmuffled engine grew, shaking tree limbs, causing leaves to fall and sending pebbles skittering. What the hell was he riding? A freight train?

Fagan stood with his hand out like a traffic cop fully expecting the biker to comply. The biker had to know what was waiting over the next rise from the red and blue flashing off the trees. With a thunderous crescendo a monstrous mechanical centaur erupted out of the depression. Fagan registered danger.

The rider wore a shiny black carapace surmounted by a black, beetle-like helmet; his right arm extended up, back, and in that instant Fagan threw himself backward over the seat of his ride, bending so far his body formed a horseshoe. The blade snicked overhead with a whistling sound.

The shriek of engine peaked and passed with a Doppler effect carrying the demon around a curve and out of sight. Fagan stood gasping and leaning on the bike. What just happened?

Some creep with a samurai sword nearly took off his head. Now Fagan knew what had happened to the Road Dog. There'd been no mention of this freak. How did the killer control his ride with his left hand? All motorcycle throttles were on the right. He could have used a throttle stop but that was insanely risky on twisty little roads like this. Unless he'd modified the bike so the throttle was controlled with the left hand. Who does that? Why? Fagan knew why. But still, the effort and for what? Effect? The vics were dead—they didn't have much time to admire the effect.

Fagan knew he was dealing with a real sicko.

Lightning flashed through the trees. Fagan tried the radio. White noise. He listened. Wind and thunder—and something else. Those shrieking cylinders. Fagan caught a glimpse of red light recrudescent through the trees.

The black biker was coming back.

Fagan withdrew his S&W, jacked one into the chamber and thumbed off the safety. He didn't think about his record or how this would look to the Firearms Discharge Review Board. The black biker had already tried to kill him. Well now he was going to get perforated.

Fagan crossed the road and braced his forearms on a branch, all but invisible in leaf and shadow.

Bring it on freak.

Red light splayed across wet branches followed by the demon eye, bike bent like a storm cellar door, right arm held high. He came right at Fagan. Fagan began pulling the trigger when it was twenty feet away and didn't stop until it was almost upon him. At the last instant he ducked and rolled and *swish!*

The blade cut through the four-inch elm like string cheese.

The giant motored over the crest and disappeared. The sound barreled away in a diminishing howl until it was almost gone.

Fagan got up, his uniform soaked. He listened. The engine—how many cylinders? It almost faded away. Almost. There. It was gone.

Thank God.

Fagan held his breath, heart pumping like a tweaker. Raw terror beat coffee every time. Fagan bent over with his hands on his knees searching for breath. No one would believe him. If he got an All Points out within the next couple hours they might stand a chance. Unless the demon biker went to ground.

Fagan headed diagonally across the road to his bike. On the other side of the road he paused.

He listened.

A tiny buzz.

It waxed louder.

Fagan saw four slugs penetrate the giant's black leather jacket. Why wasn't he dead? If he were wearing body armor why hadn't the 160-grain slugs at least knocked him off the bike? Was he jacked up on PCP?

What was keeping him up?

Lightning flashed. Rolling thunder joined the ascending howl of the killer's bike. Fagan sprinted to the Harley, thumbed the starter and took off, kicking up the stand in motion.

The motherfucker was returning for another pass, like it was a bullfight. No use trying to divine the motive of a homicidal maniac. Fagan had been a biker long before he'd been a cop. Riding a bike wasn't like driving a car—your sensory awareness was heightened ten-fold. You couldn't be bothered with chitchat, text messages or music. You needed total concentration to stay on the road. In the rain, chased by a killer.

Fagan held it just this side of panic as he goosed the big Harley up to fifty on roads that weren't designed for anything over thirty-five. He felt the rear tire slip in the corner and catch as his heart stopped and restarted, floorboard banging against the pavement sending a shockwave to his knee. Somehow he kept the 800 lb. bike upright. He headed southwest, certain the road would connect with either 123 or 38.

This can't be happening to me.

He almost laughed. It would almost be funny if it weren't so insane. Out of the frying pan into the fire. As he topped the next rise he saw the red demon eye pop over the crest eighty yards behind him. Fagan willed himself not to tense up and start shivering, consciously keeping from crushing the handgrips as he guided the heavy road bike faster than it was meant to go. He kept scraping the floorboards.

Where was 123? Where was 38? Come on, come on. The freak gained on him. Fagan looked down. He hit sixty. The giant had to be going eighty or better. By the laws of physics he should have planted himself in the trees by now.

Ahead through the trees Fagan caught a glimpse of desultory traffic—a pick-up truck, a bus. Had to be 123. Had to be.

Please God don't let this freak follow me out onto the highway.

He could see motorists switching on their wiper blades. Rain smacked and went away like a harlot flicking a handkerchief.

He was close to panic, like a small animal with a giant predator breathing down its neck. He glanced in the mirror. The demon's eye almost blinded him, a mere quarter of a football field behind. They'd taught him never to ride in a panic but no one had envisioned these circumstances.

Fagan held the throttle flat out as the big bike accelerated to ninety, crested the top of a hill and went briefly airborne, landing with a clank. The red demon eye was right behind him. Fagan heard its strange engine thrashing and humming like something at war with itself.

Fagan rushed the highway—a T-intersection—the road didn't go through. There would be no time to stop. He prayed that the relatively light-used state highway would be deserted.

A faint demented scream penetrated his consciousness. Fagan realized it was the creature itself, turned his head and the fucker was right there on the backswing. Fagan slammed his head down to the right of the tank and felt a jarring shock as something struck his fiberglass helmet. He felt wind in his hair.

Gripping the bars Fagan looked up to see the black biker hit the highway and grab two feet of air off a discarded sheet of plywood resting on a log.

Good! Maybe he broke his neck!

Then Fagan was out in the open sliding sideways like on a dirt track, struggling to keep the Harley on its tires. The sky was a mottled, shifting gray/purple with flashbulbs erupting behind screens and constant crosscurrents of thunder. The scabbed black highway was little wider than the country trunk he'd just left, wet as an otter. He crossed both lanes and the Harley's rear tire slipped onto the beat-down highway grass and Fagan put a foot down to keep it upright, twisting his ankle and juddering to a stop in sixty feet. He quickly pulled to the side of the westbound lane and straddled the bike on the shoulder.

He leaned on the bars, breath a jackhammer. He looked up and down the highway.

The freak was gone.

An insensate mechanical bellow erupted from a fire trail beyond the eastbound lane. Fagan stared in disbelief, spine shaking like a flag in a hurricane as the red eye reappeared, blinking in the brush waiting for a farm truck to lumber by.

Fagan gassed his bike feeling a high-pitched animal whine in his throat.

CHAPTER 6

THE KONGO KLUB

He thought he heard a tornado siren but he was seventeen miles out of town. It could have been the wind through the trees or the shriek in his throat. He looked ahead to where the road disappeared in mist. It was as deserted as after a nuclear disaster. What happens when lightning strikes a biker? Would the rubber tires insulate him from grounding? Not in the wet.

That was the least of his worries.

The trees on either side of the two-lane highway flickered red and blue from his light bars and red from the demon eye, engine roaring like an avalanche nipping at the Harley's rear tire. Fagan hunkered low on the bike with the throttle flat out and watched the Speedo creep past a hundred. The blazing red eye remained steady in his rearview, thirty feet back.

Some kind of intersection coming up fast—123 and 38. Fagan made the mistake of looking in the mirror and saw the upraised sword, the maniac's front wheel adjacent with the Harley's rear.

The maniac swung.

Fagan threw the bike down on its side and skidded next to it down the highway at ninety mph, his ballistic jacket, boots and helmet shredding leather and carbon fiber like cheese on a grater, the big bike kicking up sparks as it rotated and skidded. Fagan felt heat building through the carbon fiber. Slower and slower he scraped and spun until he came to a halt in the middle of the westbound lane, his bike skidding off the road to the right and striking the base of a utility pole like an eight hundred pound wrecking ball.

The utility pole, one in a series carrying power and phones to the hinterlands, cracked like a breadstick and trembled, momentarily held up by the power lines stretching in three directions. The third direction was to the one-story log cabin roadhouse with the neon signs advertising Schlitz and Dixie. "Kongo Klub" flickered in neon orange above the door.

Fagan lay on his back for a moment, staring at the roiling sky. He recognized the signs of shock. Carefully he tested his limbs and concluded nothing had broken although he'd look like an eggplant for several days. Ever so slowly he raised his head and looked around. He sat up.

His arm buckled. Still no traffic.

The maniac was gone. Fagan tried to listen but his ears rang like a school fire alarm. He had to get out of the middle of the road. A crack of pure white light struck the top of the utility pole. The thunderclap was instantaneous. Momentarily blinded, unable to hear, Fagan realized he was sitting in a pool of cold water and the utility pole was coming down.

Every joint a roundabout of pain, Fagan scurried backwards on his ass like a spider until he was out of the pool. He struggled to his feet and hobbled out of the middle of the road seconds before the pole touched down with a horrendous crackle and a cloud of angel fire that followed the downed line to the next pole. Fagan stopped at the parking lot, put his hands on his knees and searched for breath. He fell on his ass. He slapped around. He still had his pistol and radio.

He thumbed it. Of course it was dead. He went through his little rituals, feeling his arms and legs. The back of his head felt cool. He unstrapped his helmet. The sword had cut a perfect circle at an angle on the side of the crown, a monk's helmet. It looked like half a jawbreaker. He scratched his scalp.

The Harley was down but it weighed a ton and had highway bars so it still might be rideable. Not that Fagan had any intention of trying. He could barely walk. He had to talk to HQ and was pretty certain the KK had a landline, if it hadn't just been knocked down by the storm.

Fagan looked up. The clouds seemed darker and angrier like a mob working itself up to a confrontation. He scanned the road east/west once more but there wasn't a sign of traffic. They must have warnings out on all broadcast media.

On hands and knees Fagan turned toward the roadhouse. A series of faces regarded him through the steam-misted window, in and around the neon beer signs. He staggered to his feet. Five rat choppers out front, three with apes. One had a Stihl chainsaw bungeed to a cargo rack. The bikes dripped with skulls, grim reapers, Grateful Dead symbols, tiny bells, packets and ephemera. Bikers were more superstitious than gypsy wives. Three of the bikes appeared to be Harley-based. The other two were of unknown provenance.

He looked up. Smoke curled from the old brick chimney as from the College of Cardinals. As he watched the lights went out. Shouts and curses from inside.

The Kongo Klub was made of brown logs, possibly telephone poles, held together with white mortar. A railed porch ran the length of the club, about forty feet. There were a half dozen white plastic chairs and two round white plastic tables, the kind you buy at Wal-Mart. Fagan went up two steps to the stout brown door with a scratched square window smack in the center. Seconds later the sound of a generator starting up reached him and seconds after that the lights flickered back on.

Fagan heard scuffling and scraping furniture as he approached the door. He pulled it open and stepped inside. Pain radiated like a high red whine from his arms and legs. Five hairy bikers—three at a circular table decorated with empty bottles and two more at a square table in the back flipping cards. The card players were old. They would be Doc and Curtis. What was that like, to be an old biker with no health insurance, three teeth in your jaw and a stinking trailer somewhere?

The room smelled of beer, tobacco, marijuana and testosterone.

Two behind the bar—a grizzled homunculus and a fresh-faced blond who looked as out of place as a chrysanthemum in a coal bin. Eyelashes like crow's wings. Had to be fake. She wore a man's white shirt tied around her taut midriff and hip-hugger jeans. There was a tat of Gaiman's Death on her bicep. They all looked up. It would have been unnatural if they hadn't. But there was nothing natural about the forced bonhomie of the bikers doing their best to appear nonchalant.

That lasted three seconds.

The biggest biker, a slab of beef with a full beard, gold earrings and a gold tooth slammed a Bowie knife the size of a PT Cruiser into the scarred wood table causing the bottles to dance.

"MACY! WHERE THE FUCK'S MY BURGER!"

With a frightened expression the blond angel disappeared behind the bar.

All for Fagan's benefit.

The youngest, a wiry hillbilly with a Dennis the Menace cowlick and a wide grin, said in an adolescent twang, "Well look what the cat dragged in."

CHAPTER 7
THE ROAD DOGS

Fagan let his cop's gaze stop at each. The two in back were salt and pepper, looked like they were in their sixties although they could be anywhere from forty to eighty. The biker lifestyle put the miles on your face. They never looked up from their card game.

The three around the circular table glowed with malice. The man mountain with the knife was obviously the prez followed by a human fist with a shaved skull and inked neck and biceps in his late thirties. Cowlick was a gangly nineteen, pale face a constellation of zits.

Fagan dismissed them and walked to the bar, setting his bifurcated helmet down with a thump. He caught a glimpse of himself in the mirror behind the bar. He looked like a child's toy that had been dragged through broken glass and a coal mine.

"Bullard County Deputy Sheriff," he croaked. "Do you have a land line?"

The middle-aged bartender was short with bright, inquisitive woodchuck eyes and hedgerow brows. He leaned down and plopped a black plastic rotary on the scarred wood bar.

Someone had carved "Road Dogs" into the surface in elegant Gothic script. The wall above the bar was decorated with old license plates and tin signs: *The Wild One. Wild Angels. Easy Rider.*

Fagan picked up the receiver. All he heard was the rushing in his ears. He turned to the room. "Anybody got a working cell phone?"

His legs gave way and he collapsed to the barroom floor, brushing his helmet off the counter. His helmet rolled a couple feet and stopped.

The Road Hogs roared. Cowlick clapped his hands.

"What's the matter, Ossifer," Cowlick sneered getting to his feet. The leader put out an arm and Cowlick resumed his seat. The bartender scurried out from behind the bar with a glass of water. He walked with a limp, right leg with an odd kink.

Fagan felt weak as a baby bird. He half-struggled to a sitting position, leaned against the front of the bar and waited for the world to stop spinning. His luge ride down the highway had scrambled his brains. He might have a concussion. He looked around. There were cig butts on the floor and a quarter inch roach.

"Just relax," the bartender said softly with a southern accent, handing him the glass. "You had a wipeout."

Fagan drank thirstily. He nodded.

"We saw your bike slam into that pole. You nearly got your ass fried."

Fagan tried to say something but couldn't find the wind. He drained the glass. The bartender helped him to his feet and deposited him on a barstool. "I'm Fred," he said softly. "You must be the new deputy. You know the Road Dogs?" Just a hint of anxiety.

Fagan nodded. "Officer Fagan," he said.

"What's that?" the kid said standing. "Did you say Officer Faggot?!" He doubled up cackling. The others barked. A real knee slapper. Fagan thought Cowlick seemed a little manic. They all did—they all had that artificial stillness speed freaks get when law walks in the room.

By thy long gray beard and glittering eye....

Not that Fagan gave a shit, but they probably had to scrape goods and works off the tables in a hurry when he slid by. He thought he sniffed a telltale chemical tang. Fred went behind the bar and nervously wiped with a white cloth. Fagan pointed to the bottle of Jack Daniels behind Fred and held up two fingers.

"Please," he croaked.

"Hey Ossifer Faggot!" the kid sang. "Ain't it against the law to drink while you're on duty?"

The bikers watched Fagan with barely concealed mirth. This was better than a pole dance. Cowlick scooted forward and scooped up Fagan's helmet, turning to display it to his comrades like a belt he'd just won. He saw the hole in the helmet and stuck a finger through.

"What the fuck?"

The slab held his hand out. "Hand it over."

The kid flipped the helmet to the leader. "Here you go, Wild Bill."

Wild Bill examined the helmet and looked up. "What the fuck happened to you?"

The bartender leaned in. "You need something stronger than Jack, officer." He dipped below the bar and retrieved an earthenware jug with a cork stopper. Someone had doodled a skull and crossbones on the side with a black felt marker.

"This here's the real thing—genuine corn liquor. One eighty proof." He poured two inches of brown liquor into a tumbler. Wild Bill stared in fury and consternation.

Fagan held it up to the light, tossed it back and swiveled to face the room. The liquor hit his gut like a depth bomb. Heat flared in all directions. He waited a second for it to get into his blood. The room tilted and whirled.

We all need it one time or another.

Three pairs of eyes regarded him with undisguised hostility. Salt and Pepper never looked up from their game.

"What kind of pig starts drinking at four in the afternoon?" the skull snarled.

"What happened, officer?" the leader said with exaggerated unction.

"Anyone know a Lawrence Rodell?"

The kid's jaw dropped and his face twisted in shock and disbelief. Salt and Pepper looked up. They did not radiate hostility. Rather a world-weary cynicism.

"What about him?" Wild Bill said.

"He was decapitated."

Cowlick turned to the skull. "What's that mean?" he said softly.

"Means his head was cut off, numb nutz."

The bartender mouthed something behind the bar.

"Bullshit!" the leader exclaimed.

"Man on a bike," Fagan said. "Possibly seven feet tall dressed all in black leather. Full face helmet carrying a samurai sword."

"BULLSHIT!" Wild Bill declared pounding the table. "BULLSHIT! MACY! WHERE THE FUCK'S MY BURGER?!"

The graceful girl/woman sashayed out from behind the bar carrying a platter on which rested the burger, condiments and three shot glasses filled with Jack. She set the shot glasses neatly before Wild Bill, Cowlick and the skull and then slammed the burger down in front of Wild Bill hard enough to make it airborne.

Wild Bill backhanded her with his right hand, the sound of flesh on flesh like a rifle shot. Macy staggered.

Fagan got off the stool with blood in his eye.

CHAPTER 8
HELMET HEAD

Before Fagan could reach the table the skull popped up and shoved him back hard with pile driver arms. Fagan stumbled and grabbed the barstool for support taking it down with him. Fred hurried out from behind the bar and got in the skull's face as Fagan regained his feet.

"Come on, Chainsaw. I thought you guys weren't gonna cause me any grief."

"That was before this pig walked in," Chainsaw said. "How do we know he didn't off Larry himself?"

"You heard the man," Fred wheedled. Fagan felt sorry for the bartender, forced to grovel before this pack of jackals.

"He didn't do it. He's a cop for Chrissake!"

"Cops are crooked as your right leg," Wild Bill said, picking up his burger and chomping a coaster-sized hole.

"Yeah, ya fuckin' gimp," Chainsaw said. "Weren't for us you'da closed this pit long ago."

Fagan could have arrested Wild Bill for assault right there. But one did not provoke a pack of jackals. He could always charge him later.

Cowlick whipped out a bindle and a balisong and divided some lines on the tabletop. The name "Mad Dog" was stitched over one breast. His blade made a chopping sound against the wood. "You need a bump, Saw." Mad Dog bent and hoovered a line, sat back and spread his arms bodaciously with a grin of satisfaction, taunting Fagan.

Fagan swallowed. His throat felt like a diesel exhaust. He couldn't find any spit. Maybe he was having a panic attack. He was at their mercy. He dare not show the slightest sign of fear or they'd crush him. Without the stool to support him he'd collapse. His knees felt like Jell-O. He brushed the pistol at his hip hoping no one noticed.

Chainsaw slowly turned, sat at the table and rotated it on its axis until the meth lines were before him. This rotated Wild Bill's burger two feet to his left and in irritation Wild Bill grabbed the table like a big steering wheel and twisted it back just as Chainsaw's straw came down.

Wild Bill picked up his burger and lopped off another quarter. He set it down.

"You done?" Chainsaw said.

"For the moment."

Chainsaw rotated the line back and snorted. He rotated the hamburger back into place. He got up, scooping the police helmet, strode to the bar and slammed it down on top of Fagan's tumbler shattering glass everywhere. Quick as a cobra he grabbed Fagan's leather lapels and jerked him close.

Fagan drew the gun. Chainsaw shoved him back six inches and slapped the pistol out of Fagan's hand as if he were a child. He grabbed Fagan by his belt and jacket and threw him savagely to the floor.

"Larry was a Road Dog, motherfucker," he growled. "He was a friend of mine."

Lightning struck followed almost immediately by the thunderous crack. The lights flickered. Chainsaw jerked forward and kicked Fagan in the ribs with the tip of his steel-toed road boots. Fagan felt it crack.

Fred ran out from behind the bar and grabbed Chainsaw's arm.

"Chainsaw don't—!"

Chainsaw shook the bartender off and elbowed him in the face without even looking. Fred fell to the ground groaning. Fagan got to his feet, charged with his head low and took Chainsaw down amid the crunch and scrape of overturning chairs and breaking glass.

"Stop it!" Macy snapped from behind the bar with an edge of hysteria.

Fagan grabbed an empty beer bottle and brought it down base first in the middle of Chainsaw's forehead whacking the shaved skull onto the wood floor. The thug was stunned. Fagan felt a sick triumph in his gut.

Wild Bill shoved his chair back so hard it skidded into the wall. He yanked the Bowie loose lifting the heavy wooden table an inch in the air. The table banged the floor. Fagan scrambled to his feet, back to the bar, searching for his pistol while keeping his eyes on Wild Bill. Fagan grabbed the red-upholstered bar stool and held it like Jungle Jim in the lion's den.

"I'm a police officer!" he said.

Wild Bill came on like an angry mountain, lupine fangs gleaming behind his unkempt beard, blade catching bar light as he flipped it hand to hand.

"Bill!" Macy barked.

BLAM.

For an instant there was stunned silence as ears imploded from the force of the blast. Plaster fell in chunks onto the bar thinning to a steady column of dust as particles continued to trickle from the hole in the ceiling. Fred stood on a chair behind the bar cradling a truncated pump-action Remington twelve gauge.

Another goddamn felony.

Even Wild Bill stopped, blinking stupidly like a pig. His face split into a wide grin.

"Fred. I never knew you had it in you."

The bartender surveyed the room, shotgun at parade rest. His blue eyes were bright and blazing and his mouth was buttoned shut with extreme emotion.

"We all know what this is about!" he snapped. "Helmet Head."

CHAPTER 9
HERE COME DE JUDGE

"BULL. SHIT," Wild Bill thundered. "I swear, every time you bring that up...."

"He's real," Fagan said. "I saw him."

The three Road Dogs surrounded him with red faces. Rage, testosterone and a shitload of meth. Wild Bill returned his blade to its sheath.

"Spill it lawman," Wild Bill said.

Fagan told them about finding Larry's body, his flight to the bar. "None of you have ever seen him?" he finished. "He's hard to miss."

"They been telling that same stupid story for twenty years," Wild Bill said. "My old man said it was a crock of shit then and it's a crock of shit now."

"Cop said he saw him," rolled up from the back of the room. The old white biker with a prodigious belly and a beard spoke without looking up from his cards.

In the brief silence that followed Fagan heard the black man quietly say, "Gin," and lay his cards on the table.

"Sheeit."

"That's Doc," Wild Bill said, little pig eyes fixed on Fagan. "That other sorry ass fossil is Curtis. They're married, ain't that right boys?"

"Thems was in Nammmm," Mad Dog said. "Or was it the Civil War?"

Thunder rolled over the Kongo Klub like a line of caissons. Rain poured in through the shotgun hole. Macy came out from behind the bar with a big saucepan, placed it on the floor beneath the leak. She was the brightest thing in the room and clearly didn't belong there.

What was she doing in this dive? She couldn't possibly be involved with that ape, could she? Fagan hoped not. Focus, son. He was holed up in a remote roadhouse with five bloodthirsty thugs in tornado weather and a seven foot monster outside chopping off heads. Things always looked better when you put them in perspective. He tried his radio and got white noise. For all he knew Ptolemy had been flattened.

"You have a cellar?" he asked Fred.

Fred shook his head. "This is it."

"Why'd this fucker chop off Larry's head?" Chainsaw said.

"Let's find him and fuck him up!" Mad Dog chimed in.

"You dumb shits," Wild Bill said. "Can't you see he's playin' you?"

"No he ain't," the bartender asserted. He seemed to have gained courage from his shotgun blast. "How do you think my leg got messed up?"

"You told us you hit a deer!" Wild Bill sneered.

"I told you I got this runnin' from that freak and you insisted I hit a deer! You were so fuckin' drunk and stoned at the time I can't believe you even remember."

Wild Bill pointed a bratwurst-sized finger. "Watch it, old man."

"He's out there somewhere holed up in Milton's Hollow most likely. That's where he found me."

"What makes you think that, you old fool?" Bill said.

"You know about Milton's Hollow! You've heard the stories! Christ knows how many bikers he's killed they never found the bodies."

Fagan held his hands up. "Gentlemen, I'm not looking to bust anyone for drugs or any of that shit. We have a more serious situation on our hands. Are any of you carrying firearms?"

The Road Dogs looked at one another and broke out laughing. Even Doc and Curtis looked up with grins on their faces.

"They're all carrying," Fred said.

"You wanna form a posse, Marshall?" Wild Bill asked in an exaggerated Texas twang.

"A pussy posse!" Mad Dog brayed. Wild Bill and Chainsaw guffawed.

"You gonna swear us in as deputies?" Mad Dog said spraying spittle. Fagan thought he might actually be excited about the idea. "Dig it! There's five of us! No fuckin' road freak can stand up to the Road Dogs! Let's track him down and light him up!"

"Dog, you're dumber than you look," Wild Bill said. "Popo what's the deal? You're not about to deputize us."

"Just want to know what I'm dealing with," Fagan said with a straight face. "I don't think guns will stop him anyway."

"You say you gave him five in the chest."

"I hit him at least three times—I saw the perforations. He must be wearing ballistic armor."

"Like Doc!" the kid warbled. "Him and Rastus there wear helmets, too!"

Wild Bill's hand shot out like a bullwhip, smacking Mad Dog in the face and causing him to stagger. He touched the red mark and looked up like a hurt puppy. "I warned you about that shit. Curtis a charter member. You ain't even a Dog yet. You just a pledge. Don't go disrespectin' Curtis. We don't need that racial shit."

Mad Dog rubbed his cheek. "Sorry, Bill." An afterthought: "Sorry, Curtis!"

The old black man did not look up from his game.

Somewhere in the back the generator sputtered. The lights went out.

"Shit!" Wild Bill exclaimed. "What, you run out of gas?"

"Just hang on," Fred said. "I'll go check. It has plenty of

gas." He rummaged around in a drawer behind the bar and found a flashlight. Playing the beam on the floor Fred went through a door to the left and behind the bar. A sickly light played through the big front window. Fagan checked his watch. It was five-thirty—it would be light out for a couple hours if the curtain of storm held off. Thunder.

Everyone but Doc and Curtis were on their feet waiting for something. Fred to restore the generator. The lights to come back on. The all clear to sound. The wind blew hard rattling the windows and causing blinds to buzz like a mad locust. Fagan found his gun and returned it to his holster. They heard Fred cursing and shoving things around in the back.

At first it was subliminal, the sound a mosquito makes as it approaches the ear and you feel that first flash of appre-hension/irritation. It grew a little and assumed a mechanical aspect, thrashing cams and gears, an intermediate buzz, a dentist's drill, a weed whacker, pipes bellowing to fill the sky causing the floor to vibrate and bottles to migrate. Wild Bill and Chainsaw exchanged an *Oh Shit!* look. Fred rushed out of the back wild-eyed with grease on his face. He ditched the flashlight behind the bar and picked up the shotgun.

A freight train pulled up to the door as crimson light splashed blood across the walls. The thrashing built to a crescendo and fell silent. Fagan, Wild Bill, Chainsaw and Mad Dog went to the front window and looked out.

Fagan struggled to control the pain in his ribs. He didn't want them to see weakness. He looked out the window between Mad Dog and Chainsaw.

The bike was big and black, covered with so many designs, runes, plates and covers that its nature remained a mystery. The rider kicked out the stand and got off. He was big, dressed entirely in black leather with a full-face helmet. He unhooked the bungees holding a large black helmet bag to the pillion, picked it up via the top handle like a briefcase and strode toward the club.

"Holy shit," Mad Dog said, voice cracking.

The rider's tread was heavy on the steps. The boys backed away from the window unconsciously forming a semi-circle facing the door.

The door swung open.

CHAPTER 10
POOR SERVICE

Helmet Head paused in the door and looked around. The door frame cut off the top of his helmet. He stooped as he stepped inside and the door wheezed shut behind him. Water trickled off his leathers and helmet and fell from the helmet bag to the floor. He walked to the bar passing within three feet of Fagan but taking no notice. He set the helmet bag on the bar with a ponderous thump. Pinkish water leaked from the bag onto the bar top.

Fred backed himself up until he was leaning against the whiskey, eyes wide open, mouth stretched into a Dodge grill. The shotgun resided under the bar where the visitor couldn't see it. Helmet Head leaned on the bar with his hands and stared at Fred.

Fagan thought about shooting the black rider in the head but he'd already tried that and look where it got him. Nor was he certain the Road Dogs wouldn't turn on him afterward and testify against him. And then he saw the black leather sheath affixed to the rider's back. A long, gently curving black scabbard. Fagan's eyes returned to the helmet bag like a mesmerized deer.

Helmet Head extended one black-leathered hand toward the bar pointing at the bottle of Jack.

"We're closed," Fred croaked.

The featureless shield stared at him like an X-ray machine. Helmet Head straightened up and slowly took in the assembled starting with Wild Bill on his left, gaze pausing on each, serially and separately. His gaze particularly lingered on Macy who shrank back against a cabinet. Helmet Head spread both hands in an Italian gesture.

Whaaaa—?

"We're closed," Fred choked again. "These boys were just leaving." He sounded like air escaping from a child's balloon.

Helmet Head placed his right hand on the helmet bag and waggled his fingers as if pondering something. He jerked the helmet bag off the bar and headed toward the door. Just before he reached it he turned, pointing a finger at each of them in turn like counting passengers for a tour bus.

He left the bar as a curtain of rain washed over them, lashing the windows and playing a discordant tune on the shutters. The outside world blinked white followed by the crash of thunder. Wild Bill and Fagan returned to the front window and watched as Helmet Head attached the helmet bag to the back of his bike.

Macy ran out from behind the bar into Wild Bill's arms. "Oh my God," she sobbed.

"It's all right, Mace," the biker assured her. "Just a lotta show."

"You see those punctures in his jacket?" Chainsaw said. "The pig speaketh truth."

In back, Doc picked up another card.

"Oh yeah?" Fred said, grabbing his shotgun. "OH YEAH?!"

The little man hobbled out from behind the bar and stumped toward the front door.

"Fred, wait a minute," Fagan said but the bartender was on a mission from God. He ran out the front door, down the steps, toward the black rider. Helmet Head turned to face him, hands at sides palms open.

Whaaaa—?

Fred went down on one knee. "Remember me, motherfucker? *Remember me?!*"

Two blasts struck Helmet Head in the chest further shredding his expensive black jacket. The black biker staggered back but stopped himself from falling when his butt hit the bike.

Fred got to his feet dazed as if he couldn't believe what he'd just done. Helmet Head strode toward him drawing the katana from over one shoulder, passing it through Fred's neck and returning it to his back in one perfect parabola.

For three long seconds Fred stood quivering. His head slid one way and his body the other. Helmet Head stooped, picked up Fred's head with both hands like a basketball and Michael Jordaned it toward the roadhouse.

Fred's head smacked through the window like a seven pound cannonball, striking the back wall and falling to the floor spewing blood. Glass flew.

Macy screamed.

"Motherfucker!" Wild Bill exclaimed, reaching into his vest and pulling out an Arsenal double-barreled .45. Chainsaw reached down to his leather gym bag and withdrew a long-barreled .357 magnum. Mad Dog pulled a nine from his backpack and the bikers surged toward the front door like the Three Stooges.

"Hold it!" Fagan yelled, drawing his own pistol.

The black bike roared to life. Three foot gouts of flame erupted from the pipes. Helmet Head pulled out of the rain-slick lot and motored down the road, the shrieking cacophony becoming fainter until it merged with the sound of the storm.

CHAPTER 11
THE FREEZER

Fagan went out on the porch. Chaos was chaos but this was getting out of hand. The wind had tumbled the cheap - plastic chairs and tables into the wall. "Can anyone fix the generator?" he called, his voice sounding unusually loud in the absence of thunder.

"I can fix anything runs on gas," Mad Dog said turning back toward the club. He brushed by Fagan, deliberately giving him the shoulder as he went into the club and behind the bar. Fagan still felt weak and sore from his crash and that kick to the ribs didn't help.

Fagan followed him in. "Is there a freezer back there, something that will hold the body?"

"If it'll fit," the kid said and disappeared through the door.

Doc and Curtis remained at their back table playing cards.

"One of you guys help me carry the body in?"

"What for?" Doc said without looking up.

"Might be awhile before we can get an ambulance out here," Fagan said.

Curtis pushed himself back from the table. "I will."

He was a wiry black man with close-cropped steel-gray hair and beard wearing tinted round glasses. He had a diamond stud through his left ear and his brown eyes were devoid of the rage Fagan saw in the others.

Together they went outside. Wild Bill and Chainsaw were arguing, oblivious to Fred's body. Blood had poured from Fred's neck to mix with the rainwater.

Curtis stooped and grabbed the headless body beneath the arms. "Looks like he's pretty much exsanguinated."

Fagan took the bartender's boots, stitch lancing across his ribs where he'd been kicked. "You have medical experience, Mr...?"

"Curtis. I'm an RN."

Fagan led, going up the three steps to the deck. "That's a new one on me. A black RN outlaw biker."

Curtis followed Fagan into the bar. "Yeah well we don't get too many Jewish cops around here."

Fagan opened the bar door with his elbow and Curtis followed.

A thrum rose from the rear of the building. The lights flickered and went back on. Mad Dog came out of the back door grinning and slapping his hands together in an exaggerated manner.

"Told ya."

"Good on ya, Mad Dog," Curtis said as they squeezed by him into the storeroom.

Mad Dog flattened out against the wall as Fred's corpse passed.

There were two doors behind the bar at right angles. One led to the storeroom. The other led to Fred's private quarters.

Inside the store room the door shut automatically behind them. The big, concrete-floored space was lit by two sixty watt bulbs hanging from the ceiling—a fire marshal's nightmare. Stacks of Cutty Sark, Jack Daniels, Johnny Walker, Four Roses and a dozen other brands formed sentinels against one wall. A deep horizontal freezer sat against the opposite wall next to two old uprights.

"What makes you think I'm Jewish?" Fagan said, as they gently laid Fred on the floor next to the freezer.

"Knew a cat in Nam named Fagan. Tom Fagan. Told me it was a Jewish name. Plus you got that nappy hair. Plus you ain't from around here."

Curtis chuckled.

Fagan carefully went through Fred's pockets: a folding knife, three quarters and a penny, a moist blue bandanna and an old Zippo lighter with a Harley logo. He placed these items in an empty cardboard box, stood and opened the freezer. It was half full of pub food including pre-pressed burgers, frozen French fries and drink mixes. There were two upright refrigerators to one side. Fagan stuffed as much of the perishables as he could into the uprights' freezers leaving plenty of room for Fred's body.

They carefully laid it inside. It just fit without the head.

"I've seen a cut like that," Curtis said. "When some North Viet big shot wanted to make a point he'd decapitate a prisoner."

"You were a POW?"

"Three months. Then the bombers came. They fly so high you don't know they're there until the ground explodes. Seen men lose their heads to a flying tin roof."

The freezer remained open. Mad Dog bounced through the door holding Fred's head in both hands and tried to sink it from ten feet. Curtis' thin body snapped like a whip as he intercepted the pitch, hauling the head into his belly with both hands.

"You'd best get out of my sight," he said softly.

Mad Dog shimmied in mock fear and slouched out. Curtis reverently laid the head in the freezer and lowered the lid.

"There's plywood in the shed out back. Figure we should patch that window before it starts to rain again."

Fagan followed Curtis out the back door to a cinderblock supply shack. The battered red door faced the rear of the bar and was partially open. A big green dumpster crowded one side, an old Ford pick-up the other.

Curtis pushed the door open, noticed Fagan wincing. "Crack a rib?"

Fagan grimaced and nodded.

"See if I can tape it up. Might have some Vicodin." He rummaged through his denim vest, found a bottle of ibuprofen.

"Try these."

"Thanks." Fagan gratefully unscrewed the bottle, bounced four into his hand and swallowed them with a swig from a can of Royal Crown Cola.

"I'll be all right."

"Ahuh."

"You know as soon as the power comes back on this place will be crawling with cops."

"What makes you think the power gonna come back on?"

Fagan tried his hand-held. Nothing.

Inside the shack was a complete workbench with tools and a circular saw, big rectangles of plywood stacked against one wall. Fred's Fat Boy sat against the back wall covered with dust. Curtis grabbed a tape measure, a hammer and a box of nails and headed back to the club.

"You know what day it is?"

"Thursday," Fagan replied hitching to keep up.

"June 22. My momma wouldn't let me out the house on this day. Said this the night the haunts all roam. Ain't Halloween. No sir. June 22."

Back in the bar Macy sat weeping in a chair.

Wild Bill was in Doc's face. "I say we go."

"I say we wait until morning. He ain't going anywhere. You heard Fred. He lives in Milton's Hollow."

Wild Bill leaned in and sprayed spittle. "You lily-livered piece of shit. My old man should have left you in Nam."

Doc stayed calm but Fagan could tell he was ready to explode. Wild Bill abruptly turned. "How 'bout it, Curtis? You comin'?"

Curtis used the tape measure on the front window. "What about the Aces of Spade my man Terrell?"

CHAPTER 12
THE BOOK OF DEATH

Wild Bill snarled, "That motherfucker killed Larry and took the ice! He killed Fred. Likely killed Terrell and took our twenty grand. He's got our ice, our cash, and he's killed two of our friends."

Creases radiated from the bridge of Curtis's nose. "Terrell should have been here by now. Terrell is one punctual cat."

Mad Dog stared at Fagan. "Maybe the pig took the ice, you ever think of that?"

Wild Bill snorted. "You've got to be shittin' me. Look at him! Do you think he'd drag his sorry ass in here holding our ice? Well here's your chance, pig. Ride with us—help us get that Fred killer."

Macy looked up with red eyes.

Fagan measured his words carefully. "Guys, that's tornado weather outside. I advise you to stay inside until the power comes back on and we get an all-clear from the state highway patrol."

"Yeah, right," Wild Bill sneered.

"Pussyyyyyyyy," Mad Dog hissed. He laid lines out on the table top. "I told you not to trust no jigs."

"Shut the fuck up, Dog," Wild Bill said, bending to the table and hoovering a line. He looked up energized. "How about you, Macy. Want a bump?"

"No thanks."

"Come on. Maybe it might uncrank your ass."

"No, thank you."

"Jesus, Macy. You used to be fun."

Macy got up and went behind the bar where she drew a glass of water and sat on a stool. Curtis set down his tape measure and followed her. The rest of the Dogs could care less except for Doc who watched warily.

Fagan leaned on the bar. Curtis knelt next to Macy and said just loud enough for Fagan to hear, "Does Wild Bill know?"

Macy shook her head. "And don't tell him."

"How long have you known?"

"A week."

"You need something for cramps or nausea?"

Macy looked up. "What have you got?"

Went unsaid were, *do you plan to tell Bill, and what do you plan to do with the baby?*

"Please don't make a fuss, Curtis. I don't want anyone to know."

Curtis turned his soulful eyes on Fagan. Macy looked up.

"Please don't tell anyone," she said.

"I won't."

Wild Bill snorked and bellowed, "Saddle up, boys!"

"Not before we get that window sealed," Curtis said. "You ain't gonna leave your woman open to the elements, are ya?"

Wild Bill looked from Curtis to Macy with little pig eyes.

"Go a lot quicker if you guys chip in," Curtis said.

Chainsaw sprang to his feet. "I'll help you measure those plywood sheets. How we gonna cut 'em?"

"Fred's got a table saw in the shed."

Curtis called off measurements. Chainsaw wrote them down. He, Curtis and Mad Dog returned to the shed. Soon Fagan could hear the shriek of the table saw. Even Wild Bill helped mount and seal the window. Chainsaw's measurements and cuts were spot on. The replacement sheet was exactly the size of the plate glass window. Mad Dog found a tube of window putty in the shed and squeezed the whole thing out around the frame so the wind couldn't get through.

He stood back, hands on hips, proud of his handiwork. "Got any spray paint?"

"All right?" Wild Bill said. "Everybody happy?"

"That'll do 'er," Curtis said.

"Lock and load, boys."

Mad Dog pulled out his nine, Chainsaw the magnum, Wild Bill the double .45, Doc a Taurus Judge five-shot revolver chambered for .410 shotgun shells.

Curtis looked at Doc. "What the fuck, Doc?"

"Curtis, we took an oath. You saw what he did to Fred."

Wild Bill stood. "Let's roll." He looked pointedly at Fagan. "You coming?"

Fagan backed away with his hands up, palms forward as if to say, "I don't have a thing to do with this."

"Don't be here when we get back. Macy darling, make yourself beautiful for me."

The quintet trooped out of the bar shaking the floor. Fagan remained standing at the bar, Macy seated at a table with her face in her hands. Seconds later the Road Dogs' bikes exploded into five kinds of thunder, revved, gassed, goosed and shredded down the road.

For a moment there was silence. The room was much darker with the plywood in place. Macy looked at Fagan with red-rimmed eyes. "Fred kept a book."

"What book?"

"About the killings." She pushed the chair back with a screech, got up and went behind the bar. She went into Fred's private quarters and returned a moment later with a big vinyl scrap book covered with dust, the cover plastered with a peeling Grateful Dead logo and a Harley decal. She stood behind the bar and smacked the bar top with it causing a mini dust storm that rolled over an ant. Macy flicked the ant off the bar top with a finger, flipped the book open to the first page and turned it toward Fagan, a yellowed newspaper article clipped from the *Carbondale Courier* dated June 20, 1999.

CYCLIST BEHEADED BY GUY WIRE

State and local officials have declared the death of Chicago native Robert MacGruder to be the result of a first-degree homicide. They believe the 48-year old motorcyclist was beheaded by guy wire stretched between trees in the Shawnee National Forest.

Sheriff Jonah Brach of Sharon County said the killing bore similarities to a five-year-old homicide, the unsolved death of motorcyclist Wayne Cappucio. "We may be dealing with a serial killer," Sheriff Brach stated, asking that anyone with any knowledge of either case to please contact his department.

Fagan's throat dried up. "Could I have a glass of water please?" he rasped.

Macy filled a bar glass with water and handed it to him. He drank it all, handed it back. She refilled it.

"How is it possible nobody knows about this?" he said. "Why isn't this a big deal?"

"Nobody gives a shit about outlaw bikers."

Fagan wondered if Sheriff Fullerton were incompetent or merely ignorant. From the way he talked, Fagan always assumed Fullerton was from around these parts. How could he not mention this?

How could he not know?

Fagan had interviewed for the job three months ago. It had taken them that long to make up their minds.

He turned the page. A story from the *Harrisburg Gazette* about a biker found with his head lopped off only this time the killer left the head. Some grad student riding cross country. Dartagnan Broddus was a history major and Civil War buff. Police were looking for "an historical re-enactor, possibly with a Confederate cavalry sword."

Someone with deep-seated racial prejudice.

Broddus' family offered a five thousand dollar reward for information leading to an arrest. Fagan had a feeling there had been no arrest. Coming from a medium-sized city Fagan understood the politics of unsolved cases. After awhile they became an embarrassment which the higher-ups simply wanted to go away. Maybe the killings had stopped for awhile. Fagan flipped ahead—there were only two more entries, the last from 2008. Four killings in all. Not exactly an epidemic.

Unless there were others that had gone unnoticed.

Macy had a point. No one cared about a bunch of hoodlum bikers whose life expectancy was equivalent to that of some Third World country.

"Are you really a cop?" Macy said.

Fagan showed her his badge and ID card.

Macy picked up the ID card, her face twisting in consternation. "It's your fourth day on the job?!"

"Ma'am, this looks like a criminal conspiracy to distribute meth."

Macy's mouth dropped open in a half guffaw. "Are you for real? Don't you think we have other stuff to worry about?"

"Sooner or later power will be restored and so will the rule of law. Do you have any outstanding warrants?"

"Who, me? No."

"Do you know if any of the others do?"

"I'm no snitch."

"Does he often lay hands on you like that? I should have arrested him for assault. I would be happy to do that."

"Yeah right. And get the shit beat out of you."

"I'm looking at a criminal conspiracy. Sooner or later they're going to restore power in Ptolemy and I'll be able to get through on my radio."

"You want to know about me and Bill?"

The wind picked up. Thunder rumbled. The lights flickered.

Macy buried her head in her hands and sobbed. Before he knew it Fagan found himself on the other side of the bar with his arm around her shoulder. She stood and let him embrace her.

"Bad, huh?"

CHAPTER 13
TAPE

Macy grew up in Kinney, Iowa, second child of Herbert and Rosalyn Edwards. Kinney lay seventy-five miles south and west of the Quad Cities. Herb was a Farmer's Insurance agent. Rosalyn was a stay-at-home mom. Rosalyn was unhappy. She could never quite put her finger on it. She saw a therapist and a yoga instructor.

She had an affair with the yoga instructor. She broke it off when she became pregnant for the third time, when Macy was five.

Shane was five years Macy's senior, the Firstborn, the golden child. He was a remarkably handsome little boy who liked to twist kitten's tails until they squealed. When the folks weren't looking he would wipe his boogers in Macy's scrambled eggs or pour Tabasco into her tomato juice. He shoved other children at the playground. Macy always knew there was something wrong with him.

He turned Marcy's childhood into a grueling ordeal. But things were going to get worse. Much worse.

She was eleven when Shane held her down and penetrated her with a vibrator he'd stolen from a house party which he'd crashed.

She was so overcome with shame that it never occurred to her to approach her parents, the police or a counselor. She had sex with those boys to see if she could, to see if it was different. Not much. It wasn't until years later, and Wild Bill, that she achieved an orgasm with a man.

All left unsaid.

She went Goth in high school as a form of camouflage. Fagan blanched when she described her Goth Barbie dolls with their Mohawks, piercings, homemade tats, wounds and vampire fangs, but Macy didn't notice. She built a Shane doll from a Ken and systematically amputated his limbs.

She graduated somehow and went onto Carlton School of Nursing in Wexfordshire.

"In my junior year at Carlton I worked summers at Don's Malts, Shakes, Burgers and Dogs on Lake Nebagamon near Wexfordshire. This guy I knew took me to the drive-in to see *The Wild One*. Man, it knocked me out," she told Fagan. "Then one day the Road Dogs roared up. Most of my regulars took off like wildlife fleeing a forest fire.

"Wild Bill just looked so beautiful to me. So young and charismatic. I was so naive. He had me on the back of his Harley within three days. My parents nearly died.

"I suppose I was looking for a father figure. My real dad and I didn't get along."

Her mother still prayed for her return and called her every Sunday but lately the calls had become listless as if both parties understood she was gone for good. Hooking up with Bill did little to further her career. She thought she was in love. Bill told her he ran a successful motorcycle shop and owned his own home which turned out to be a shotgun shack in Carbondale.

He made his money dealing drugs. Within six months Macy had a cocaine habit and was reduced to staying in the shotgun shack stepping on the product until Bill realized how far gone she was and took that away. Locked her in a room and made her quit cold turkey.

"He fed me cold turkey sandwiches. He thought it was funny."

Once she cleaned up Bill sent her out to find a real job.

Against overwhelming odds she got hired as a receptionist for an ad firm in Moline and was doing great until Bill showed up one day, drunk, stoned, buzzed with a bee up his ass about how she loaded the dishwasher wrong and started wanging her around the reception room.

Cops were called, Bill was arrested, charges were dropped, Macy lost her job. She declined to press charges. At least she no longer had to explain the odd bruises or dark glasses. There followed a series of unsatisfying jobs which she lost through hard luck or Bill. His record was remarkably clean for such a scumbag.

She'd been with him for four years. Like victims of the Stockholm Syndrome, she regarded his abuse as normal, even a sign of love. She was obviously ambivalent about the baby.

"How old are you?" Fagan asked.

"Twenty-six."

"You want to think about testifying against him."

She gave him that half-guffaw look. "Are you nuts? Do you know how vindictive he is? It's a way of life with Bill. He'd find me and have me killed."

"Not if you went into witness protection."

"Oh mannnnn," she said stopping to drain a glass of water. "Are you for real? Where are you from anyway?"

"My last job was with the Duke County Sheriff's Department in Iowa."

"What'dja do to end up here? Screw the captain's wife?"

Fagan felt the color rising. He turned away and winced.

"What? Did I strike a nerve? Chainsaw broke a rib, didn't he? You want to take your shirt off let me have a look?"

"Do you know what you're doing?"

"Two years nursing school. Not much you can do for a cracked rib but tape it up and take pain meds."

Fagan peeled off his jacket and shirt revealing a hairy chest with a gold Star of David dangling from a thin gold chain.

"Raise your arm."

Macy examined the purpling bruise where Chainsaw had sunk his Size 10 Doc Marten. "Yup," she said, poking it. Fagan winced.

"That's gotta sting."

"Yeah, thanks a lot."

Macy giggled. "I'll be right back."

Fagan examined his surroundings. The TV hanging from a bracket above the bar was off but the bar lights were on including several strings of Christmas tree lights which cast a gay glow on the antique mahogany back bar. Fagan figured someone had put them up at Christmas years ago and never bothered to take them down.

There was a stuffed bobcat above the bar. The pine paneled walls contained a bulletin board advertising odd jobs, baby-sitting, puppies and so forth. There was a dart board at the far end of the room and a cold jukebox beneath a horizontal side window, an old sprung sofa backed into a corner against the front wall where some booths had been ripped out. The unpowered jukebox looked like an Easter Island head. Shelving high up on the south wall held a couple dozen souvenir steins, the kind with the hinged lids and intricate ceramic design. Dusseldorf. Heidelberg. Munich.

Macy returned with a bottle of rubbing alcohol and a spool of tape-backed bandage. She pulled a seat up next to Fagan who guessed that this was not the first time she'd been pressed into service as a nurse.

Of course the Road Dogs traveled with their own MD and RN but they seemed such an odd group. Doc and Curtis were quiet, self-contained with a certain inner peace that eluded the others.

Fagan grunted as Macy applied the alcohol to his ribs and to his forehead.

"Nice goose egg you have here."

Fagan craned his neck to look at himself in the mirror behind the bar.

"What are their real names?"

"William Hedgecock," Macy replied without looking up, intent on applying the bandages to minimize rib movement. "Chainsaw is Derek Gunderson, Mad Dog is Sam something, I never did catch that. I don't like him. Doc is Tom Garrison and Curtis is Curtis Jones."

"What are Doc and Curtis doing with this bunch?"

"You heard Doc. They took a pledge. They take this thing

very seriously. Doc and Curtis are original Mad Dogs. They started the club along with Bill's dad Ed back in the seventies when they got back from Nam. It all goes back to Nam."

"Doc, Curtis and Ed Hedgecock were in Vietnam together."

"That's right. Ed died in a motorcycle accident when Bill was fourteen but by then the die was cast, as they say. Bill waited six years to make his move then declared himself president. Some of the other Road Dogs bitched about it but Bill whipped them into line, so to speak. Doc and Curtis didn't give a shit. They're not in on the drug running and so forth."

"What are they doing here?"

"I don't think they knew this was a drug run."

Fagan found her proximity extremely disturbing. She wore some delicate animal scent, small high breasts tapering into a slim waist. He shifted around to hide his erection. He hadn't had a woman in months, not since before the incident. He sucked it in until she finished taping then stood half turning away.

"Is there a shower back there I can use?"

"Sure. Through the door on the left."

Fagan moved stiffly to take a cold shower.

CHAPTER 14
THE APPLICANT

The interview took place on March 13. Fagan arrived at the Bullard County Courthouse, which also housed the sheriff's department, at nine-thirty sharp wearing a new suit from Men's Warehouse, bright and eager as any young FBI hopeful. He wore a tiny American flag in his lapel.

He waited in the antiseptic-smelling reception room for twenty minutes. The magazine selection included *Law Enforcement Weekly*, a Farm & Fleet catalog, and a six-month old issue of *Entertainment Weekly* with Johnny Depp on the cover. Depp was made up to resemble Betsy Ross in a new movie about the American revolution. Fagan didn't know it was Johnny Depp until he read the fine print.

The sheriff opened his office door from behind the divide and leaned out. "Fagan?" he boomed.

Fagan stood. "Yes sir."

"Come on in."

The middle-aged receptionist buzzed him through the gate and he followed Fullerton into the office, which looked out on the back parking lot. Fullerton was six-four, handlebar mustache, wore a Stetson and affected a good ol' boy style. His .44 revolver lay in its leather holster on a sideboard.

"Have a seat," he said, sitting behind his gunmetal desk and picking up Fagan's resume and file. He looked and he looked. He used silence as an interrogation technique.

Fagan waited patiently.

"You ride a bike?"

"Yes sir, all my life. Right now I have a Yamaha 1100."

Fullerton resumed his perusal.

"Says here you and the Duke County Sheriffs' Department agreed to part ways. Doesn't way why. You want to fill me in on that?"

Fagan stifled a sigh. "It was political."

"Ahuh. I called Sheriff Gruber and he told me he was not at liberty to discuss it. We're a small department, Pete. It only works if we all work together. You'll be off on your own most of the time but I need someone who knows how to be a team player."

"Sir, I think my military record speaks to that."

"So it does and I appreciate your service to our country. Thing is, I'm wondering why a guy with your experience would even consider working for a Podunk outfit like ours for the magnificent sum of $48,000 a year."

Fagan smiled and spread his hands. "I love the open road. I love to ride. I love all the twisty turny little farm roads you've got down here."

Fullerton peered at him squint-eyed for awhile. "I get the feeling there's something you ain't tellin' me. That's all right. We all got secrets. Fact is we need a man who's independent, who can talk to country folk, someone who understands that the produce has to get to market on time. Someone who knows the difference between a star high school athlete who's maybe had a little too much to drink, and some no-account trash looking to get high and steal some citizen's wheels.

"I guess you know we got a meth problem. Some of these kids break into abandoned structures and use 'em for meth labs. Sad to say, there are quite a few abandoned structures in Bullard County. These past ten years ain't been kind to us. Some folks are growin' marijuana. I know Zeke Elkins is doing it but damned if I can find the grow. Some folks are buyin' cigarettes off Injun reservations and running them up here to beat the tax. We get a lot scammers through here every time there's a tornado, offering to fix roofs, houses, etc, taking old folks' money. My rural dep has got to get to know these people and understand them."

"Sir, I'm gregarious and I understand folks. My father was a Rabbi."

"I wondered about that. You left your religious affiliation blank."

"I'm not much of a Jew, sir. My father was a reform Rabbi. I was adopted."

"Well I ain't much of a Christian to tell you the truth. I try to be. A man's faith is his own business. But that's interesting. You have a religious education?"

"Like I said, my father tried. Faith is a gift."

"Ain't that the truth."

Fagan thought back to all those Saturdays and Sundays spent at Temple school learning about the great Jewish scholars, the history of Judaism, the Old Testament. Like a caged animal, desperate to bolt that den of stultifying boredom. Looking back on his childhood Fagan reflected it was long stretches of boredom punctuated by seconds of stark terror. That was also pretty much a description of war or police work.

How could he explain what had been on his mind for those seemingly endless hours? He was deeply ashamed of his childhood obsessions. While his father taught of God he dwelled on evil. When his father pointed to the great spiritual leaders, he conjured monsters in his head. He entered a period of darkness where he could easily have gone either way. It lasted until his enlistment.

He stalked women. He was a peeper. He vandalized property.

Fullerton weighed Fagan's application in one hand. "Son, ever now and then I play a hunch. Now you and I both know there's a lot unsaid here about why you left your last job but I'm not going to press you on that. For some reason we didn't get a whole lot of qualified candidates and I need someone now. Will you be ready to start by June 17?"

"Sir, I'm ready to start now."

"Make any difference whether I use the *Old Testament* or the *New Testament*?"

"No sir."

Fagan reached behind him to a bookshelf beneath the window and placed a red Rosicrucian's Bible on the desk. Fullerton stood and took off his hat. Fagan stood and placed his hand on the Bible.

"Do you solemnly swear to serve the citizens of Bullard County, the Constitution of the United States, to uphold the law without fear of favor?"

"I do."

"So help you God?"

"So help me God."

Fullerton pumped Fagan's hand. "Welcome to the force. Now there's a few things you need to know...."

CHAPTER 15
TRAFFIC STOP

It was really the Rabbi's own fault Fagan became a biker. The Rabbi took young Pete to the annual Memorial Day parade and hoisted young Pete to his shoulders. From this vantage point Fagan watched the baton twirlers, the Homecoming Queen and King in their borrowed Sebring convertible, the Mayor in a borrowed Corvette, the 4H, Junior Achievement, JayCees, Boy Scouts and Girl Scout floats, local radio and TV personalities. And then came the Shriners on their mini-bikes. A bunch of fat old men in purple fezes zipping in and out of traffic, performing breathtaking chicanes and not acting their ages.

From that moment on all the Rabbi heard was, "Can I get a mini-bike?"

To which the answer was an unequivocal no.

However, the Rabbi's neighbors the Thompsons had just such a mini-bike, and young Ralph Thompson was not shy about burning up and down the block. Fagan sat on the curb and stared intently. He wanted to ride that thing so bad he was seriously considering knocking Ralph off his perch and just taking it.

Fortunately Ralph was a generous boy. He showed Fagan

how to work the controls and turned him loose. Fagan ran out of gas forty-five minutes later down by the tracks. Ralph soon followed on his bicycle. Fagan ended up pushing the mini-bike two miles home. He was thirteen.

No matter where he rode his one-speed Huffy the wind was against him. It was against him as he pedaled to school in the morning and it was against him when he pedaled home at night, the weight of his backpack pressing between his shoulders.

Someday, he vowed, he would own a motorcycle and not have to do all this fucking pedaling.

In his fourteenth year Fagan grew four inches and stopped thinking about mini-bikes. Now he wanted a motorcycle. The Rabbi laughed.

"After you're on your own, you can get a motorcycle. But not while you're living under my roof."

Fagan haunted the local dealers: Suzuki, Honda, Yamaha, Kawasaki. The town wasn't big enough to have a Harley dealer. He became a paperboy for the *Chesterton Bugle Courier*, rising at five a.m. each day to deliver the paper with a thump to door stoops all over town, seven days a week. He told the Rabbi and Esther he was saving for his college education. He wasn't sure they bought it, but they were pleased with his discipline. In the summers he took jobs mowing grass.

On day he was mowing the Sanderson lawn on Lake Wyandotte. It was a lazy Sunday morning with water skiers and sail boats out on the lake. The mower sputtered and died by an old elm. Out of gas. In the sudden silence Fagan heard chirping and noticed a distressed robin hopping on a branch, taking off, doing little loops and landing in an agitated manner. He looked down. A hatchling had fallen from the next and was squirming in the grass.

Fagan's first impulse was to crush it with his heel. But something about the desperate mother's exertions attracted his attention. He'd heard somewhere that the scent of human flesh on a baby bird would doom it to abandonment so he trekked back to the garage for a can of gasoline and a roll of paper towels. Back at the tree, he gently picked the baby bird up in the paper towels and deposited it among its mates in the nest, which was eight feet off the ground.

He hopped down, fueled the lawnmower and resumed his job.

He didn't realize until much later that it had been a tipping point.

Fagan turned fifteen on August 15. The Rabbi wouldn't let him get a learner's license. "Do we look like farmers to you?"

For four hundred dollars Fagan bought a well-used 250cc Yamaha dirt bike, no title. No license. Couldn't ride it on the road. Did anyway. He kept it at his friend Josh's house. There was so much junk in the Peterson garage no one noticed.

All went well until Fagan did a one and a half gainer off a hidden log in the woods and planted his face in the earth. He came home with a huge shiner, limping. Somehow he convinced the Rabbi and Esther that he'd had a mishap swinging on the rope which hung over the lake.

One evening in September the Rabbi had a speaking engagement at the First Evangelical Church of Spartanville, about fifty miles away. He asked Fagan to accompany him and help lug the audio-visual material. The topic: "The Survival of Israel and the Chances For a New Holocaust in the Middle East."

They were running late. The Rabbi stepped on it, pushing the old Volvo station wagon to seventy-five on the state highway. Out of nowhere, lights and sirens appeared behind them. It was like that scene in *Close Encounters of the Third Kind* where the UFOs show up at Terri Garr's rural home. Whamo!

Chagrined, the Rabbi pulled over to the side of the road. Fagan stared in awe as the trooper got off his big police Harley and sauntered over, book in hand. The Rabbi wore a black suit and tie. The rear seat was jammed with Bibles, Torah, research materials. There was a Support Your Police sticker in the rear window.

"Sir, do you know why I stopped you?"

"Yes, officer. I was exceeding the speed limit. I have no excuse."

"You in a hurry?"

"I'm late for a speaking engagement at the First Evangelical Church in Spartanville."

"This your boy?"

"Yes sir. Say hello, Pete."

"Hello, officer."

"You clergy?"

"I'm a rabbi."

The cop examined the Rabbi's license and registration. He handed them back. "How about I escort you into town, and after this, you stay within the speed limit, Rabbi? That all right with you?"

"Yes sir. And thank you, officer."

Fagan lit up like a Saturn booster launch. His eyes had seen the glory. The seed was planted. If the Rabbi had any idea his son wanted to be a cop, let alone a motorcycle cop, he might have moved them all to Israel.

CHAPTER 16
HOT DOG

F agan's only friend and partner-in-crime was Josh Peterson. They met in the 7th grade, phys ed pariahs. Josh was the Fat Boy. Fagan was the concave-chested wraith. Josh was the original gun nut. His father was an avid hunter and Josh knew all there was to know about guns. He had access to his father's rifles and pistols. With the bullying Josh endured, it was a miracle he didn't pull a Columbine. He never expressed a wish to blow his tormentors away.

They would borrow Josh's father's rifles, go into the fields and blast away at anything that caught their interest. One day Josh loaded dum-dums into his father's scoped 30-06. Rifles over their shoulders they hiked through the fresh April fields to a tree line. Josh sited down on a crow in a tree.

"Watch this."

He squeezed the trigger. The crow exploded like a feather bomb and the sudden report launched a dozen others into the air cawing. Josh handed the rifle to Fagan.

"Here. You try it."

They walked down one side of the windbreak until they spotted a squirrel sitting in a tree. Using the crotch of another tree to steady the rifle, Fagan sighted in. The fat squirrel loomed large in the cross-hairs. Fagan squeezed the trigger and the squirrel exploded into fur and flying meat. Birds took to the skies.

"Gimme the rifle!" Josh enthused. "I see a barn cat!"

Josh's most prized possession was the Waffen SS dagger he got from his grandfather who fought in the Battle of the Bulge. The boys would huddle in Josh's basement bedroom poring over pictures of the Third Reich, goose-stepping around and yelling in bad German accents. Fagan knew well the horror of the swastika. Maybe it was his id crying out, *I am not a Jew!*

Fagan worked at a local country club as a caddy one year. Myron McDonald was the Head Caddy. He liked to punch Fagan in the arm as hard as he could.

"Levi!" he roared. The other caddies roared with him. It was the height of wit.

Fagan and Josh watched horror movies. Fagan's taste ran toward *Godzilla, Gojira, Anaconda, Tremors.* Josh favored torture-porn: *Saw*s I through V, *Hostel*s I through IV, *Last House on the Left.* They sneered at *Star Wars* and referred to their adherents as "stookies."

It was Josh who turned Fagan on to comics. Fagan had always regarded them as silly. The only ones he'd seen were *Archie* and *Richie Rich.* Josh showed him what was happening at Marvel and DC, characters like the Punisher or Hellblazer. *Ghost Rider* in particular intrigued him. The idea of a flaming motorcyclist. If Fagan had to be a superhero, he would be Ghost Rider. From there it was but a hop skip and a jump to the EC crime comics of the fifties, which Josh owned in hardbound. He bought them himself from money he earned from his paper route.

Fagan could not believe the lurid tales of suffering and vengeance and they fired his imagination in all the wrong ways. Josh showed Fagan his father's secret stash of *Playboy* and *Oui.* The only reason Fagan didn't start his own collection was fear of the Rabbi. The Rabbi was the personification of kindness, but his disapproval was like a lead blanket.

Josh had a younger sister named Adrian who was a brainiac and ran interference for him at home. She was plain, wore glasses and had an instinctive sense of how to cruise under the radar.

Josh's parents gave him a Volkswagen Beetle on his fifteenth birthday. Farm kids could get a permit at fifteen. Josh and Fagan would drive around looking for small game to blast.

Once when Josh stopped the car to take a shot at a barn cat in a barnyard, the farmer saw him and rushed out of his barn clutching his own shotgun. Fagan hadn't thought a VW could burn rubber like that.

After that he declined Josh's hunting trips. They still spent plenty of time together. Despite his predilection to shoot animals, Josh was a good friend, kind and generous. His size disturbed him but he couldn't control himself. He ate like a starving dog. Saturday night's they'd cruise to the Dog & Suds on Main Street and park in the shadows to watch the cool kids flirt, blurt, roll and testify. Fagan usually got the meal from the pick-up window as he was less likely to attract attention.

"Hey there's Faggot with his friend Big Pussy!"

"Hey Faggot! How you two love birds doin'?"

Fagan often wondered why they subjected themselves to that ordeal. He was aggressively, obsessively heterosexual but like most boys his age didn't have the slightest idea how to score a girl. Silently acknowledging each other's hopes and longings, Fagan and Josh never discussed girls except to express their disgust when someone they liked started dating someone they didn't.

Fagan kept his peeper phase to himself. Staring through blinds, saving the images up for when he was home alone in his basement lair. With the monster models and torture devices.

The Rabbi wouldn't permit video games in the house but Josh had plenty. He loved *Grand Theft Auto* and *Call of Duty*. He'd sit in front of his computer for hours blasting away with remarkable accuracy. He was the only person Fagan knew who trained for video games on real firearms.

They ate together in the school cafeteria. Once a week the school served hot dogs. When this happened, the muscled and mulleted Myron McDonald, a thug who fancied himself a wit, would lay in wait for Josh, swoop down unexpectedly, pluck the hot dogs from Josh's plate and stuff them into his face like a wood chipper. All the time smacking his lips and spraying spittle.

One day Josh took a glass tube from chemistry class and inserted it into one of his hot dogs. The look of shock on Myron's face was like the sun rising over the Pacific. From Vietnam, obviously. After consultation with Josh's student adviser, students and parents (Mr. Peterson was, after all, a veteran), it was decided that Josh would be suspended for a week.

McDonald was a well-known troublemaker tolerated for his athletic prowess. The principal talked McDonald's parents out of pressing charges, pointing to the fact that Myron himself was open to numerous bullying charges. Young Fagan had volunteered to detail numerous instances of anti-Semitic behavior and of course the school system could not tolerate that.

Josh returned to class in October. For Halloween, Josh and Fagan planned to dress as a mad scientist and deranged assistant. Josh was the idea man. Josh called the shots. He would be the mad scientist although they both knew that in reality, that is, in the fictionalized reality of horror movies, it would be the little guy Fagan playing the mad scientist and Josh the hulking assistant with one finger up his nose.

Josh procured an outsized white lab coat with a hacksaw sticking out of one pocket. He greased his hair into a huge pomp like a wave about to break and wore thick glasses with adhesive tape around the bridge. He lovingly splattered the lab coat with red paint. He carried a black leather satchel which contained a six-pack of Coors and a couple of joints.

Fagan wore an OshKosh B'Gosh coverall, had made his face up with putty and fake blood to expose scavenged canines, fake stitches and carried a garden spade over his shoulder.

They weren't trick or treating. They were too old for that.

They weren't going to any parties. They hadn't been invited.

They were just going to cruise Main Street and enjoy the scene.

They arrived at the Dog & Suds at eight-thirty and the streets were chock-a-block with trick-or-treaters from the very young, ferried from house to house by their parents, to teenagers with backpacks full of soap and toilet paper. Josh parked his car at the back end of the lot out of the lights and in the shade of a molting locust tree.

Fagan waited in line behind Freddie Krueger. When it was Fagan's turn he ordered three hot dogs and two root beers from Buffy the Vampire Slayer. As he returned to the car he saw Mullet-head Myron and his evil sidekick Claude Owens leaning over Josh's windshield shaking a can of spray paint.

Outraged, Josh burst from the driver's door and reached for the can of paint.

"Stop it!" he howled.

Myron slammed his fist into the big boy's gut doubling him over and causing him to go to his knees. Claude Owens, who wrestled varsity and looked like a big pink boar laughed and kicked Josh in the ass sending him sprawling.

"Help me," Josh cried pathetically.

Fagan threw a hot dog. It hit Myron on the back of the head, startling him into turning, looking at Fagan, then down at his feet where the hot dog lay.

"Did you just throw a hot dog at me?"

Fagan dropped the food and ran. He ran through the parking lot, across the alley, behind the feed store, and didn't stop until he lay gasping with pain lancing through his side behind the Piggly Wiggly, a bolus of self-loathing lying in his gut like concrete.

Myron and Claude didn't bother to pursue but the next day the tale of his hot dog and subsequent flight earned him a new nickname. Hot Dog.

Fagan and Josh drifted apart.

Years later Fagan heard from a friend that Josh had died of AIDS in New York.

CHAPTER 17
MOTOR

Storm clouds turned Milton's Hollow chiaroscuro as the five bikes cruised in tight formation. Wild Bill led followed by Chainsaw, Mad Dog, Doc and Curtis. Chainsaw frequently rode side-by-side with Wild Bill oblivious to the threat of oncoming traffic.

Doc and Curtis hung thirty yards back, also riding side by side. Each carried a first aid kit and Doc also carried a medical bag. He wondered what the fuck he was doing there. Wild Bill had told him that it was just a beer run, hang out with Fred for a few days maybe run over to the river and do a little gambling.

Then when they got there, they had to wait for Larry who was bringing down a couple ounces to tide Wild Bill, Chainsaw and Mad Dog over until Curtis' friend Terrell from the Aces of Spade showed with two keys.

Neither Doc nor Curtis did hard drugs. They smoked a little reefer and drank a lot of Jack. When Doc asked Curtis how the fuck he could sanction a two key deal, Curtis shrugged and said he had nothing to do with it. Wild Bill went over his head.

The Road Dogs met the Aces of Spade in Biloxi the previous year. Curtis had gone to school with several of the

Aces in Memphis where he'd grown up. By the time he reconnected with them he was already a Road Dog.

Doc and Curtis met in Nam where they were both medics. After they got back Doc went to medical school on the GI Bill and worked a series of small hospitals in the Upper Midwest until he found a secure berth at Our Lady of the Redeemer Hospital in Vermillion, SD. It was a good fit. Doc was raised Catholic. Those nuns used to kick the shit out of him. They were some tough babes but he learned reading, math, and science. He may have learned critical thinking. The jury was still out.

Nothing like a six-foot Nunzilla with buffalo breath and a steel ruler to inculcate young minds in the sciences.

Doc hadn't been to confession in fifteen years. He didn't miss it. Bikers had zero sympathy for whiners or hand wringers. If you couldn't put the past behind you you had no business riding with the pack.

He'd done bad things in Nam. So had Curtis. But they'd changed. They weren't the crazy young studs they used to be. An Army priest brought Doc through one of his blackest times. If it hadn't been for Father Darby he probably would have eaten his gun.

Doc's first wife was certifiable. He had the worst luck with women. The better looking they were the crazier they were. The break-up with Astrid was brutal and dragged on for months. His lawyer was bleeding him dry and still he could not come to a settlement. She thought she'd married a lifetime paycheck. But as an itinerant physician working on contract at mostly Native American hospitals he was barely able to keep pace with his school loans. Finally, one day, his lawyer said, "Whatcha got left?"

"My pick-up truck."

"Give me the pick-up truck."

So Doc gave the lawyer his pick-up truck and just like that the divorce was final.

He'd had two marriages. Both ended in smash-up, but his daughter Brigid by his first wife loved him and ran her own business in Seattle. His old lady Doris was watching Doc's two mutts. They were so old they croaked.

Doris was a stacked, forty-something realtor in Midlothian specializing in industrial properties. They'd met at a bike show at the McCormick Center. She rode a Shadow 750. It was love at first sight.

His father George had been a physician. Also an abusive prick. His mother Lucille drank herself to death. Astrid herself died of a combination of booze and oxycontin, which she took for her fibromyalgia. There were always a million things wrong with her. As a physician, Doc couldn't get to the bottom of any of them.

His second marriage wasn't much better but at least the woman lived.

Doc took Zoloft, Flomax and a half dozen other prescription drugs because he was a stupid old man who couldn't shake his biker habit. As long as he could remember it's all he wanted to do—belong to a cycle gang. It was a genuine miracle that he'd achieved this without killing or maiming anyone, or being killed or maimed himself. Of course the night was still young.

Doc was a founding father.

He and Curtis and Ed and Davis.

Doc was drafted. Curtis, Ed and Davis signed up.

Davis was a scrawny Crip from Compton. He'd enlisted to get out of the hood. He'd never ridden a motorcycle but after seeing *Wild Angels* in the mess the idea took hold like a visit from Jesus. He walked around with his hands curled around invisible grips making motorcycle noises. When the sergeant called him over, he said, "Just a sec, Sarge!"

"Ring-ding ding ding," he down-shifted through four gears before coming to a complete stop with a salute. They called him Motor.

They'd been working together up country for two months and on one crazy hot raining night punctuated with thunder and gunfire they'd promised each other that if they made it back to the world intact they'd form a biker club called The Mad Dogs, after their company nickname. This was before Ed became a tyrant. Ed was Olaf from *The Blackhawks*. Ed was Dum-Dum from Sgt. Fury's *Howling Commandos*. Ed was Bulldozer from *Easy Company*.

It was called "Operation Thunderbolt," a guerilla-like raid to disrupt supply lines going to North Viet regulars who were already in the south at division strength. M Company, aka "Mad Dogs," consisted of twenty-two men, Lieutenant Grazio in charge, four sergeants and the rest grunts. They set up camp on top of a rocky knoll near Pharpang, a village of several thousand that had fallen under VC control. The VC lined up the mayor's entire family and machine-gunned them to death for cooperating with Saigon.

Late in the day Grazio sent six sappers including Motor to booby-trap the trail with Claymores and fougasse drums.

Doc and Curtis thought Grazio was a punk and made the wrong call. Grazio was a glory-hound. Grazio wanted medals. Grazio thought he was T.E. Lawrence. The sappers should have waited until morning. It was a mistake to send them out that late in the day. They ran into a VC patrol and got bogged down in a firefight. Grazio compounded his mistake by sending ten men to pull the sappers out, including Ed, Doc and Curtis.

Technically they weren't required to bear arms but they weren't about to sit around while their buddies were getting chewed up. Ed split the patrol into two groups of five. He led the one with Doc and Curtis. Sgt. Hoyt took the other squad. Ed led them a difficult route just below a ridge that ran north/south and stuck up like a dorsal fin. The land was mostly vertical, sharply creased green valleys formed via ancient volcanic action followed by receding ocean. Snakes and poisonous insects lived in the rich green fur of the tropical rain forest.

Curtis, who fancied himself a chef, developed several snake recipes. He talked about opening a restaurant in New Orleans, Snakes Alive, that would serve snake, alligator and other reptiles, along with more traditional fare. "You put enough hot sauce on it, anything taste good."

It rained. Like walking under a warm waterfall. Doc and Curtis concentrated where to place their heavy jungle boots. A mistake could send them plummeting to the bottom of the ravine collecting every plant, bug and snake in the way. They'd heard about a corpsman in Tango Company who'd slid down a ravine and been bitten in the crotch by a pit viper. His testicles swelled to the size of softballs before he died.

There was also the killipede, a millipede the size of a hot dog with a bite so poisonous it made your eyes explode.

Ed wore camos and a campaign hat, his vast green bulk nearly invisible in the rain. Suddenly he raised his hand. The column stopped. He motioned Doc and the rest forward. They huddled on the treacherous path as the rain poured down, ten feet beneath the knife-edge summit.

"There's something down there," Ed whispered indicating the crevasse. "See that flash of red?"

The boys squinted through the rain. Doc caught a glimpse of an unnatural crimson and winced. "I'll go," he said.

Rigging a line to one of the wiry little trees, Doc rappelled down the steep incline using gloves, thirty feet to a small plateau jutting over the rushing stream. His boots sank into the red mud. Davis sat with his back to a tree, his head in his lap. The flash of crimson was his neck.

CHAPTER 18
ED STEPS UP

Doc froze. The body could be booby-trapped. He tapped his radio. The Cong would have difficulty pinpointing the patrol in this weather, even if they knew where he was.

"I found Motor," he said when Ed answered. "They cut off his head."

"We'll be right down," Ed answered.

"Hang on. Let me check it out."

On hands and knees Doc examined Davis' body looking for trip-wires or anything that didn't belong. Davis' dog tags hung from the white bone tip of his spine. Someone had placed it there. Doc examined them minutely before deciding they were unconnected. He scooped them up and put them in his pocket. Thank God he didn't have to write the letter. Everyone liked Motor. He sang Smoky Robinson in an uncanny falsetto.

The rain eased. Hell broke loose. Slugs ripped the riot of undergrowth inches above Doc's head. He recognized the distinctive whine of AK-47s. VC patrol laying in wait. Maybe they got tired waiting. Maybe they couldn't see through the undergrowth and rain. Doc hit the ground flattening himself as much as possible. Bullets ripped through his rucksack, each a hammer blow to the soft pack but missing his flesh. He was trapped in a fire zone.

From up above fire rained down. The boys were shooting blind. They couldn't see shit in this weather and the Cong were using flash suppressors. Doc couldn't stay where he was. He slithered forward and down, following the contour of the narrow valley as it broadened and flattened slightly near what had once been a creek and was now a fast-flowing river. Doc became one with the rich black mud. It was in his hair, his nose and his mouth. He welcomed it. The mud helped conceal him from his assailants.

Due to the fact he had not been hit Doc concluded the Cong were guessing. There was no way he could rejoin the team. They were up there. He was down here. He just hoped they didn't get suckered into a cross-fire.

Muffled reports exploded like Lady Fingers all around him but mostly up the slope. Doc got his back against a tree and slowly got to his knees, scanning the hillside for heroes and villains. He wished he had one of the new infra-red night scopes even if it did weigh five pounds. By now it was evening and the natural light was fading. A nerve-grating bird shrieked with metronomic regularity. Doc wanted to shoot it.

He saw a flash of gunfire high on his left. Cong in a tree. Fixing the place in his head he raised his M-16 to his shoulder but did not use the sites. He triangulated hand, muzzle and eye and fired thrice at the place he thought he'd fixed. There was a grunt and the sound of something heavy crashing to the earth. Score one for triangulation.

The firefight intensified upslope where he'd left the patrol. Someone grunted and the shooting stopped. Doc heard a babble of Viet. The VC were closing in. In the rain and jungle he couldn't tell from what direction or how far.

Sweat rolled down his back in rivulets. He pulled out his canteen and drank greedily. He set the M-16 down and pulled his .45, standing with his back to the tree, both hands wrapped around the handle.

Dear God get me out of this. I swear I'll live a Christian life. I'll devote myself to the less fortunate. I will sing Your praises 'til I die.

He thought about the bike he planned to get. The new 1200 Electra Glide. Fifty-eight horsepower. Four-speed transmission. It was his rocket ship to freedom. Doc spent almost as much time dreaming about motorcycles as he did about pussy. He'd mount a windshield and leather saddlebags and ride that sucker to Alaska and back. Just thinking about it made him feel better—the cool breeze, the endless vistas. Moose. Alaskan Thunderfuck.

He'd get an old lady—one of those Minneapolis ice princesses—a skater—she'd sit pillion and rub her titties against his back mile after mile. Just thinking about it gave him a boner.

Hard metal poked him in the side of the head as a steel gun butt smashed his hands causing him to drop the .45. Two Cong had sneaked right up on him, one on either side. The one with the AK jabbed him in the guts with the butt and pointed for him to get down on his knees. Shaking, Doc complied. The other grabbed Doc's gun, held it up smiling, kissed it, stuck it in his black canvas pants which were held shut by a bungee cord.

The Cong couldn't have been out of their teens. They looked like children. One of them wore a Cap'n Crunch T-shirt. The other wore a Boston Red Sox shirt. They grinned and chattered fast and soft in Vietnamese. He knew they were going to kill him.

An iron fist squeezed Doc's heart. He lost control of his bladder, grateful that no one noticed. A terrible sucking void opened in his chest. This was it. He wasn't ready to go.

Dear God not yet.

Grinning, one punk drew a Makarov and leveled it at the center of Doc's forehead.

The explosion was louder—much louder—than Doc expected. He waited to be dead. A second explosion and the other teen Cong dropped to the ground, swinging his rifle.

Ed separated himself from the fronds holding a smoking .45 in one hand, covered with mud, face filled with still intensity. He'd slid on his ass down the side of the mountain.

"Motherfuckers," he spat drawing his machete. Doc watched while Ed hacked the heads off both the VC. He switched the heads and looked from one small corpse to the other. "Still can't fuckin' tell 'em apart."

CHAPTER 19

TERRELL

There were times Doc missed Ed. Wild Bill didn't become such a dick until after Ed died. Not that Ed was a bed of gardenias. He should have stayed in the military. He would have lived longer.

Once they got the club going—charter, clubhouse, constitution, original members—Ed embraced the biker image until it was only a matter of time before he killed himself. He drank more beer, snorted more meth, chased more pussy, administered more beat-downs and rode faster than anyone else. He declared himself a flaming wreck not long before he became one.

The charter: "The Mad Dogs Motorcycle Club is hereby formed for the purpose of fermenting (sic) brotherhood, camraderie (sic), and motorcycle riding. We, the undersigned, constitute the Founding Brothers of this MC."

The charter went into 37 pages of details regarding name, trademark, by-laws, prospects, new members, responsibilities and chapters.

The boys pooled their money and bought a defunct Texaco station in Midlothian, IL. There were nine original members:

Ed, Doc, Curtis, Tony "Numbnutz" Nunzio, Tommy G, Arlen "Iceman" Shrum, Donnie Downer, Ricardo Z, El Indio and Larry "Red Rocket" Rodell. They furnished the place in Student Cast-Off. Some of the sofas had to be fumigated. No prob. Ricardo Z worked for Orkin. They put the sofas in giant plastic bags and gassed them.

They used the engine bays to work on their bikes and the occasional car. They gutted the office and sat around an old conference table Ed bought from a start-up that went belly-up. The place wasn't so much decorated as filled with the junk and whimsy of its members. Rat Finks, *Hustler* spreads, pictures of bikes, newspaper clippings and tiki dolls decorated the walls. The place reeked of beer and cigarette smoke.

Ed knocked up his old lady Beatrice in 1980. Beatrice was inked like a boxcar. She worked in a bar. She was on the heavy side but then so was Ed. Wild Bill was born April 2, 1981. Everyone assumed he'd changed his actual birth date so as to avoid ridicule.

Now Ed was in the earth and Wild Bill led the club. No one knew what happened to Beatrice, not even Wild Bill.

Ed died on June 29, 1997. He crossed the centerline on Illinois State Highway 51 around eleven thirty at night and ran head-on into a Mack truck carrying a load of Leinenkugel. It was ruled a righteous death.

Ed was returning from scouting out a possible charter club in Paducah and had been riding with the Pounders when he got a call from his current old lady Tiffany claiming to be pregnant. Turned out to be a false alarm.

Speed and alcohol may have been involved.

The old days. They had some good times, too. One night they were all sitting around drinking and smoking reefer. The joint passed to Numbnutz, who sat in an old overstuffed chair claimed from Student Moving Days. After awhile Wild Bill looked up and said, "Where the fuck's that joint?"

Everybody looked at everybody else. "Numbnutz had it last," Doc said.

Numbnutz looked around in surprise. His hands were empty. The seat cushions began to smoke. The seat cushions burst into flame. Numbnutz rose up and out like a Titan booster. "Fire!" he cried.

Everybody tossed their beers on the chair dousing the fire.

The old days. Doc shook his head.

Wild Bill, Chainsaw and Mad Dog disappeared around a curve and Doc and Curtis instinctively slowed down. They'd always enjoyed riding together. With the others, not so much. Especially when they got to snortin' and drinkin'. Doc playfully goosed his modified Road King and surged ahead. Curtis was about to do the same when a vibration, the merest flicker of movement, stayed his hand.

A deer bounded from the trees. Curtis automatically squeezed the front brake and pushed the rear brake with superb control so as to avoid locking up, stopping a foot short as the startled creature gave one frightened look and bounded into the trees on the opposite side of the road.

Doc saw it in his rearview and immediately pulled over, shutting off his bike and getting off. He approached Curtis grinning.

"Need to change your underwear Curtis?"

Curtis pulled over and got off. "Mother*fucker*! I almost T-boned that sumbitch."

Doc pulled out a cigar. The forest was silent as if the Road Dogs had disappeared into a tunnel. Silent save for the distant rumble of thunder.

"If you had, we'd be eatin' venison for supper."

Curtis stomped into the ditch, hands on hips, mad at himself. He gazed into the woods. Old habit. He did not merely gaze, he saw. There was something unnatural about the silhouette of a tree about fifty feet in, as if it were occupied. He parted branches with his hands.

"Where you goin'?" Doc said.

"Back here. I see something."

Muttering and smoking Doc followed Curtis into the brush. A green curtain of *déjà vu* settled on his shoulders and he shivered despite the warm weather. He never suffered from PTDS but he knew guys who had. He often dreamed about Nam but not when he was awake. He wasn't one of those guys who had "flashbacks."

He was having one now.

That shape, that fucking shape in the tree. He pulled the five-shot.

"What?"

Curtis didn't answer. He stood stock still staring up. Doc pushed wet branches out of the way and joined Curtis in the clearing. A man hung upside down from a branch to which his ankles had been bound with his own shoelaces. The body faced the tree, lifeless black arms hanging down, upside down Aces of Spade patch. Memphis.

The corpse was headless and a large brown stain covered the ground where it had exsanguinated.

A bare-bones Knucklehead with a rigid frame and bobber fenders lay on its side as if it had been casually tossed there, leather saddlebags partly splayed, clothes and toiletries spreading.

"Terrell," Curtis said. "I knew this was a bad deal."

CHAPTER 20
SNAKE BIT

Rolling thunder approached. The boys had noticed Doc's and Curtis' absence and had turned around to find them. Seeing Doc's and Curtis' bikes by the side of the road they pulled over and headed into the brush.

Wild Bill was the first to step into the clearing, eyes sweeping past the headless corpse and doing a massive double-take.

"Is that our ice?" he asked

"That's Terrell," Curtis said with finality.

Chainsaw and Mad Dog entered the clearing and stood as if in awe of an original Robert Williams painting. Mad Dog had a sickly little smile on his face.

"Well did anybody search his saddlebags for the ice?" Wild Bill asked as if lecturing stupid children. Doc and Curtis looked at one another.

Chainsaw strode to the downed cycle and rummaged through the saddlebags throwing out underwear, a box of condoms, a rain parka, energy bars, a copy of *Tits* and a tin of Altoids. The other saddlebag held nothing of interest.

Wild Bill turned back to the corpse which hung from the

limb like a ghastly piñata. "It might still be on him. I mean, this is obviously that motherfucker's work and he doesn't look like a gangbanger to me. I'm betting he doesn't give a shit about dope. All he cares about is lopping off heads."

"Why do you suppose he spared us back at the Klub?" Doc said.

Wild Bill rounded on him. "How the fuck should I know? Maybe he didn't want to get his ass blown off. There were five of us not counting the cop."

"Useless as tits on a boar," Mad Dog brayed. No one laughed.

"You saw what good Fred's shotgun did," Doc said. "Seems to me he wasn't afraid of us. Curtis, you think he was afraid of us?"

"Can't say as I do."

Wild Bill snorted in contempt. He ran a fat finger under his nose. "Mad Dog, get your ass up there and cut him down."

Mad Dog looked at the corpse with disgust, back to Wild Bill and leaped for a low hanging branch from which he swung his legs over, pulled himself up branch by branch until he was adjacent with the corpse's ankles about ten feet above the ground. He whipped out his balisong with an added fillip and sawed through the shoelaces. The corpse fell to the ground with a dull thud.

Doc looked at Curtis. That was unfortunate. They should have caught the corpse. It brought back unpleasant memories.

Mad Dog hung from a branch like an ape and dropped, springing up with a grin.

Wild Bill pointed with his chin. "Search him."

Mad Dog's grin evaporated but he knelt without hesitation and went through the corpse's vest finding two cell phones and some change. Mad Dog reached across to search Terrell's left front pants pocket and jerked back screaming, hand trailing a foot long gray/green snake with a moiré pattern.

Mad Dog whipped his arm wildly trying to snap the snake loose to no avail. Its fangs sunk deeply into the meat of Mad Dog's palm. He danced around swinging his arm.

"FUCK! FUCK! GET IT OFF!"

Sighing, Doc walked over and shoved Mad Dog to the

ground. He landed on his seat. Curtis came over and put his hands on Mad Dog's shoulders. Doc pinned Mad Dog's hand to the ground, withdrew his Kershaw which opened with a flick and sawed off the serpent's head. The snake body thrashed for an instant and then was still.

Doc pried the snake's jaws apart and removed it from Mad Dog's hand like pins from a cushion. He squeezed the palm to force out more blood. "Suck on it," he said.

"That's what I told her," Chainsaw said.

Mad Dog was crying and snot poured from his nose. "FUCK! AM I GONNA DIE?"

"Eventually," Curtis said.

"Not likely," Doc said. "That there's a grass snake. They don't usually bite people 'less you're stupid enough to put your hand on 'em. Now if that had been a copperhead might be a different story."

"I feel dizzy," Mad Dog said.

"Maybe you shouldn'ta drank five beers and snorted all that meth," Curtis said.

Mad Dog looked set to spit but Wild Bill was within striking distance.

"Quit acting like a little bitch," Wild Bill said. "Fuckin' snake bite won't kill ya."

"Hell," Doc said. "Curtis and me used to eat snake in the bush."

"That's right," Curtis said. "You fry them suckers up in a little sesame oil and some mama-san chilies, mmm-mm. Them's good eatin'."

Mad Dog hyperventilated. "Shit! Now my pants are wet."

Doc watched Curtis stifle himself and grinned. Curtis wasn't a loudmouth like Mad Dog. Never had been. One of the reasons Doc and Curtis got along so well is they could keep each other's company for hours without saying a word.

"If you're through crying like a baby," Wild Bill said, "go on and finish searching the dude."

"He ain't got no wallet, Bill," Mad Dog said.

"Look around. Maybe he dropped it."

"He didn't drop it," Curtis said. "Terrell kept it chained to his belt like y'all."

Mad Dog looked again. "Pant loop been ripped out."

"So he wants the heads and the wallets."

"He didn't want Larry's wallet," Doc said. "Cop had that when he came in the Klub."

Chainsaw stared at the headless stump. "What you think was in that helmet bag he was carrying. And now he's got Terrell's. What's he doing with all these heads?"

"Heads, wallets and ice," Wild Bill said. "Maybe this spook ain't no spook at all. Maybe he's one fucking smooth operator."

Doc barked.

Wild Bill ignored him. "Maybe this is all a front for him taking over the meth trade around here."

Doc puffed his stogie until it was the brightest thing in the world, clamped in a big grin. "Five minutes ago you were telling us he wasn't interested in the ice."

"Yeah?" Mad Dog snarled. "He ain't no spook! He's just some fuckin' jamoke in body armor! Drill him through the helmet see how he survives!"

"Now there's an idea," Wild Bill said. "But first we have to find him. Fred said he lived somewhere in the hollow. We keep lookin' until we find him."

Curtis shook his head and looked at the ground. "I got a bad feeling about this."

Wild Bill snucked and ran a finger under his nose. "You and Doc been acting like a couple of blue-haired old ladies since we got down here. My advice to you is to stop whining and grow a set."

"Man up!" Mad Dog jeered.

Doc's pupils contracted behind his tinted glasses. He slowly stepped in front of Wild Bill and looked up. "Excuse me?"

Wild Bill breathed stankbreath on Doc. "You heard me."

"Night comin' on, tornado weather, we're running around like chickens with our heads cut off...."

"Exactly," Chainsaw said.

"BUK BUK BUK!" Mad Dog clucked at Doc.

Wild Bill and Doc stared it down.

"Chill," Curtis said. "We're gonna need every hand if we're gonna beat this thing."

Wild Bill looked up. "So you in?"

Curtis nodded. Doc mouthed what the fuck.

"We took an oath, Doc. Terrell was a friend of mine."

"Okay," Wild Bill announced. "Here's what we're gonna do. We're gonna slow way down and scan both sides of the road. Every time we see a gate or a dirt road we're gonna stop and check it out. He's gotta be in the Hollow."

"Hollow's nine miles long," Chainsaw said.

"What else we got to do?" Wild Bill said. "You guys are always braggin' on how bad you are. Now's are chance to prove it. Now's our chance to write the Road Dogs into *his*-store—ee. Let's go."

CHAPTER 21
NAZIS

Fagan showered in Fred's old rust-stained stall with a chip of soap and a mini shampoo from Best Western. He dried himself with a Harley towel. He went into the bar owner's bedroom and took a clean T-shirt from Fred's highboy. It said, "STURGIS, '96" and showed an Indian chief with an extravagant bonnet riding a chopper through the Black Hills. Fagan looked at himself in the tarnished mirror above the dresser. His short hair looked like a Brillo pad. He had a goose egg that looked like an eggplant emerging above his left eye.

Fagan stood in the doorway and scanned the room as he'd been trained to do.

Sooner or later he would have to go through it searching for any evidence related to Helmet Head. But now was not the proper time. He quietly shut the door and returned to the bar in control of himself. Macy had backed her chair into a corner, sitting with her arms and legs crossed as if trying to take up as little space as possible.

She must have felt it, too, Fagan realized; a crimson tide rising up his neck.

"Does that old pick-up out back run?"

"Yes."

"Do you know where the keys are?"

"Should be behind the bar."

"Can you find them for me? There's no reason for us to hang around here."

Macy got up and went behind the bar. She opened cupboards beneath the bar and rummaged. Fagan heard pots and glasses banging and clinking, shoe boxes filled with junk being shuffled. She stood, opened the cash register with a ding and removed the change tray. She picked the heavy register up by one side and peered underneath.

The bar didn't even have an electronic credit card scanner. It had one of those old-fashioned slide operators.

She turned around and faced the bar. A series of small drawers ran the length beneath the marble top and above the open shelving holding bottles of liquor. Macy went through them methodically from left to right. Fagan watched her every move, throat dry from the sight of her shifting glutes.

Stop it, he told himself.

How unprofessional can you get? Had he learned nothing from his mistakes?

On a night like this the rule book was out the window. He felt as if he'd left Planet Earth for an unknown dimension. He chuckled.

Macy looked at him in the mirror and smiled. "What?"

The smile transformed her like sun breaking through clouds.

Fagan hummed the theme to *The Twilight Zone*. "Do do do do ... do do do do."

"Peter Fagan, a sheriff's deputy in the Southern Illinois," Macy said in a surprisingly deep baritone, "with no more sense than a tripping gerbil, thinks he's on the verge of a big meth bust when he is really about to enter the Twilight Zone...."

They laughed. Macy continued looking. After a few minutes she threw her hands up in despair. "It could be anywhere. Maybe it's in his shop or his bedroom."

"I'll do it," Fagan said out of long habit. Technically the whole bar was a crime scene and if the room was to be searched he preferred to do it as he'd been taught.

Macy headed for the old sofa in the corner. "I'm going to lie down."

Fagan eased himself upright feeling the tape tug at him and returned to Fred's bedroom. There was an unframed poster of a hot chick straddling a chopper on the wall next to a similarly themed calendar, which was stuck on March two years ago. Telling himself he was only searching for the truck keys Fagan went through the clutter atop Fred's bureau: an overstyled knife, a black leather Harley wallet attached to a chain containing forty-eight dollars in cash and one Citibank credit card. Fred's license was up to date in Bullard County. A peeling jewelry box held a selection of cheap gaudy biker jewelry: sterling silver skull rings, a couple of earrings. Brass knuckles.

Fagan couldn't remember if Fred wore earrings. He hadn't been paying attention. He should have noticed.

Fagan quickly went through the dresser drawers finding women's lingerie and a snub-nosed .38 in a cigar box with a box of Federal cartridges. Was there anyone at the Kongo Klub who wasn't packing?

Maybe Macy.

In the bottom drawer beneath neatly folded T-shirts lay an old spiral notebook. Fagan pulled it out and opened it. Fred wrote in block letters like a child.

June 20. Stuck in the fuckin' ER at Bullard County Med Center. Right leg fucked all to hell. I told the ambulanse peeple I hit a deer cause I tell them the truth they mite try lock me up. I was riding thru Milton's Hollow 9:30 last night when I saw a big red headlight in my mirror. Before I knew it this freak was rite next to me trying to chop at me with a fucking sword. I knew who it was. I heard them rumors but I never beleeved them. I beleev them now. Helmet Head is real. I hit the ditch to avoyd getting chopped and that's how I broke my leg. He woulda come back too excep right then a car came by and they phoned the hospital.

That was the only entry. Fagan closed the spiral pad and replaced it in the bottom drawer. He opened the closet and found a complete set of leathers, chaps, vests, blue workshirts, jeans and a collection of boots. Fred had been a surprisingly neat housekeeper for a bachelor. There was a worn gray sports jacket. Fagan methodically went through all the pockets picking up another five bucks in change but nothing of interest.

He sat on the double-sized bed. The night stand held an ashtray, and a stack of magazines: *The Horse, Hustler, Back Yard Choppers, Tits and Ass* and a lone copy of *National Geographic* featuring "Miscellaneous Marsupials Indigenous to Outer Australia."

Fagan pulled open the drawer. Cigs, matches, Cue-tips, a bottle of K-Y, a baggie of reefer and some Zig-Zag rolling papers. Fagan pulled out the papers. Proof positive Jesus was a head. There he was on every package of Zig-Zags smoking a joint. Fagan sat on the bed and looked around the room, seeing what Fred saw. There was one small north-facing window and a lurid Harley rug made out of some cheap synthetic. A Harley blanket covered the bed. "No Cages," it said. It was Harley's latest advertising meme. Fagan laughed. A car was not a cage. It was a vehicle. You could always dive out the open windows. Bikers loved their slogans.

Live to ride, ride to live.

If you can read this the bitch fell off.

Fagan looked under the pillow. He got down on his knees and looked under the bed. Four books were stacked among the dust bunnies. He stretched and fished them out, sitting down on the bed with the books in his lap.

Hitler and the Occult, The Occult Roots of Nazism; Secret Aryan Cults and Their Influence on Nazism, and *Secret Agent 666: Aleister Crowley, British Intelligence and the Occult.* The first book was marked with a torn piece of paper. Fagan opened it to the mark. "The Spear of Destiny."

As a struggling artist in Vienna, Hitler became obsessed with the Grail legend, Parsifal, and undertook a study of the supernatural powers of the Spear of Destiny, so named because it had been used to pierce Christ's side as he hung from the cross and was said to have great occult power. Possession of the spear meant the power to rule the world. Its loss meant immediate death. Hitler later said that he learned all he needed to know about ruling modern Germany from this period in his life.

Fagan looked at the bookmark. It was a piece of 8 1/2 by 11 foolscap from an office printer marked "Property Bullard County Library System."

"Both *Guernica* and the 1934 drawing conceal references to a mystical battle between Picasso and Hitler in connection with the Spear of Destiny. This hidden pictorial narrative, set in the context of Wagner's opera *Parsifal*, reveals some uncanny associations with events in Hitler's life and with his quest to dominate Europe.

"On 12th March 1938, the day Hitler annexed Austria, he arrived in Vienna a conquering hero. He first port of call was to the Hofmuseum where he took possession of the Spear, which he immediately sent to Nuremberg, the spiritual capital of Nazi Germany.

"At 2.10 on 30th April, 1943, during the final days of the war, after considerable bombing of Nuremberg, the Spear fell into the hands of the American 7th Army under General Patton. Later that day, in fulfillment of the legend, Hitler committed suicide." (http://web.org.uk/picasso/spear.html)

Fagan closed the book.

Fagan sat there with the weight of the books on his lap. The weight of history. Old books by the look of them. Two had Dewey Decimal markings on the spine.

He had checked *Hitler and the Occult* out of the library when he was a kid. He and Josh. It had nothing to do with his Jewish upbringing. It came from someplace outside and deep within, a wellspring of self-loathing and creeping sociopathy.

His parent's heroes were scholars and crusaders. The Rabbi marched with Jesse Jackson. He had a black-and-white photo of a mob scene in New York; himself circled in red felt-tipped marker about three persons from the Reverend. RFK, Rabbi Hillel, Elie Wiesel, Sandy Koufax, Mark Spitz, Slapsie Maxie Rosenbloom, any Jew in the arts, sciences, academia or professional sports. Especially sports. Jewish sports heroes were few and far between. Kirk Douglas, Joseph Wiseman and Frank Sinatra. The Rabbi especially loved Sinatra for his efforts to break down social barriers by insisting that Sammy Davis, Jr. be part of the Rat Pack. And God love Sammy Davis, Jr.

Many an evening the Rabbi and Esther spent listening to Sinatra on the stereo, sometimes slow-dancing to Fagan's acute embarrassment. They particularly liked "I've Got You Under My Skin."

Fagan had a basement bedroom in the modest blond brick ranch style on Morton Blvd. The house always smelled of his father's aftershave and boiled cabbage, a big hit in Esther's kitchen. That and Mrs. Paul's Fish Sticks. "Jews don't know from fresh fish," the rabbi explained.

Fagan's basement room was finished in faux knotty pine covered with the objects of his desire: Cameron Diaz, Keira Knightley, Kawasaki, The Creature From the Black Lagoon. He had to keep the hard stuff hidden, not that the Rabbi and Esther ever looked too closely. That was a good lesson for the civilized—not to look too closely.

He had his own bathroom.

His model shelf contained Frankenstein, Dracula, Alien, the Wolfman. He'd scratch built his own pit and pendulum out of balsa wood and razors. His little torture devices included a scale-model gurney with a Barbie doll strapped down, hair shaved, the mad scientist standing over her with a miniature chainsaw. He made the mad scientist out of the ever popular bulging-eyed "troll" doll. Inspired by Josh he'd started his own comic collection. He had his own TV and VCR. He kept his stroke books and porn films in a box behind the furnace. He'd left it all behind when he'd enlisted. These were objects of fascination for the depraved and adolescent, not adults.

When Fagan returned from his deployment the models and pornography were gone. He and his father never commented on them. He'd attended enough of the Rabbi's lectures to know the litany. He'd seen *Triumph of the Will*, *Night and Fog*, and the Nuremberg Rally. He'd seen *Judgment at Nuremberg* and *Schindler's List*.

He looked at the books. Just an old biker's imagination? Bikers loved Nazi paraphernalia, although it had become more subdued of late as even bikers realized the impact of really bad publicity. Fagan's stomach growled reminding him he hadn't eaten in six hours. It sounded like voices from another room. He

picked the books up and returned to the bar, walked over to where Macy lay on the sofa and set the books on a bar chair.

"Have you seen these?"

Macy sat up, picked them up one by one and stared in astonishment. "No. I stayed out of his room. What's he saying? That that thing is some kind of Nazi monster?" She started shaking. "What if it comes back?"

Fagan sat next to her and put his arm around her. "He's not coming back. And I don't believe in ghosts or freaky supernatural shit. He's just a man in body armor. A homicidal maniac."

Macy shrugged him off and put a little distance between them. Fagan flushed with shame. *What was he thinking?*

"That goose egg is nasty. I'll get you some ice."

"Stay. I'll get it."

Macy stood. "No. You stay. You look like you're about to drop. I'll be back in a jif."

Fagan watched her sashay behind the bar and cursed himself for his thoughts.

CHAPTER 22
THE BOOGERMAN

What was I thinking? Macy castigated herself as she opened the door to the storeroom. Hormones! Young, good looking cop standing up against Bill. And let's face it. Bill was no longer the dashing young rake he once appeared to be. He'd put on forty pounds of beer belly and turned into a sour, abusive troglodyte who treated Macy as chattel.

She'd been thinking of getting out for a year but how to do it? You didn't just walk away from a control freak like Bill. You had to have an exit strategy. Find a replacement. Pray for Bill to jam himself up and go to prison, but even then she wouldn't be safe. Bill bragged about his extensive connections behind bars.

She'd thought about faking her own death and moving far away, but where would she go? How would she do it? She was no Jason Bourne. She had no savings. She couldn't very well appeal to her parents, not after she dropped out of nursing school to be with Bill. They had financial difficulties of their own. If she went back there Bill would know where to find her. And why would they protect her now? They never had.

A tiny part of her brain prayed that Bill would splatter himself all over the highway but her good Christian upbringing jumped on that like a hawk on a June bug.

Shame!

She'd imagined a thousand scenarios: Wild Bill dead in a shoot-out with the police, with rival gangs, with Doc and Curtis. Wild Bill dead of an overdose, heart a mushy softball from years of abuse. Kidney failure. Bad bad *bad,* but she couldn't stop the thoughts from coming.

She'd had a bellyful of Wild Bill. And how she had a belly full of Wild Bill. Well, not yet. It had not begun to show and wouldn't for a month or two. Time enough to grapple with that decision. As a little girl, she'd never pictured herself as a mother. She was always the heroine of heroic fantasies, the equal of her romantic partner as they rode into battle laughing, on their valiant steeds. Substitute a Harley for a horse and what have you got?

She'd tried praying, drowning out her thoughts with scripture. But the thoughts wouldn't stay away. How many times had she dreamed of a white knight to save her from the ogre? Stop it, Macy, she told herself. She was thinking like a schoolgirl, like one of those simpering idiots that devoured *Us* magazine and ended up in a beef with her ex on *Judge Judy.*

As if!

The cop was not a knight and Bill was not an ogre.

The baby changed everything. She had yet to see a doctor but she'd tested herself. Now it was no longer just her. It was the baby, too. Macy had no illusions that becoming a father would change Wild Bill—he already had two whelps with some woman in Biloxi who had filed for child support. Now Bill had to stay out of Mississippi. Big whoop.

He used to joke about his baby mama's futile efforts to get some relief from him. Not to Macy. To the boys when he thought she wasn't listening. Doc had a daughter in Seattle and Curtis' boy was in Afghanistan.

Bill would want her to get an abortion.

She paused inside the cavernous storeroom and shut the door behind her. It was such a relief to be alone! She lived with Bill in a trailer park across the river from Paducah. Bill's ego left little room for her and her meager possessions. She frequently spent the night on the sofa in the bar after cleaning up when Bill wasn't around. She preferred it to the chaos of the trailer.

"Ice," she said. Ice for the cop.

And here was another problem. Before things turned really bad Shane had taken particular delight in scaring the bejeezus out of her with an original creation he called the Boogerman. Despite the light-hearted title Boogerman was nothing to sneeze at.

Shane would creep outside her window at night and drone in a weird old crone voice, "The Boogerman is coming ... the Boogerman is coming...."

Macy: "DADDDIEEEE!"

Dad: "SHANE STOP SCARING YOUR SISTER!"

Shane would wait in the basement for hours giggling, knowing that their mother would sooner or later ask Macy to fetch something from the freezer. Macy was afraid of basements and dark places. She would tentatively enter the unfinished basement staring at the freezer against the far wall working up her nerve.

For Shane, timing was everything. He waited until she heaved a little sigh of courage and started across the floor before leaping out from behind the furnace wearing a sheet with eyeholes screaming, "BUGGA BUGGA BUGGA!" And then chase her, trying to rub his boogers in her hair.

The memory of her shock and fear caused Macy shame and bile in her stomach. Shane lacked the gene which made families love one another. Maybe her parents failed to pass it on. She didn't know. Maybe her mom's drinking and dad's obliviousness was an infection that killed love. She remembered being loved as a child. She felt secure pretty much up 'til five. Things began to change in grade school. That's when her parents' unhappiness with each other began to manifest itself.

Mom's drinking.

Dad's affairs.

Mom's retaliatory affair.

Macy started turning her Barbie dolls into zombies. She blackened their eyes, worked gaping wounds into their fresh skin, dressed them in rags, fabricated bones, stripped their hair and replaced it with purple Mohawks. She found solace in the goth

lifestyle. She was cursed with sunny good looks. She dyed her hair black to her parents' horror.

Shane was always there to take the heat off.

Until Macy dropped out of nursing school Shane was the black sheep. Now they were both black sheep although she, at least, was still in touch with her parents, however tenuously.

Younger bro Bruce was a CPA with a firm in Sioux City. She had always thought of him as a cipher, staying in his room playing with computers. He always sent her a card on her birthday. He was married now with a two-month-old baby.

Shane was a bad kid. She knew it, her parents knew it, and his teachers knew it. Their childhood had been punctuated by encounters with angry parents whose children Shane had bullied, teachers he'd humiliated, motorists he'd egged or stoned.

He did a little dealing, a little stealing. There was always a football or basketball coach to plead his case—until he flunked out his senior year. When he was nineteen a judge gave him a choice: Son, you can serve your country or you can serve your time. The family breathed a sigh of relief when Shane chose the Army. Be all that you can be. Shane would have despised Doc and Calvin as weak old losers but they'd come out of the Army with something resembling character.

Last year Macy learned that Shane had gone AWOL while rotating stateside. No one had heard a word from him since.

She hoped never to hear from him again. She didn't care if he were dead. In fact she wished he was dead. Did that make her a bad person?

"Ice," she said again. The sound disappeared like a pebble in a well. She went to the refrigerator on the left, an old Frigidaire with a top freezer. She opened it up. Inside were Fred's venison steaks and chopped venison meat from last fall. The whole thing. She opened the refrigerator to its right, an Amana with a side freezer. The automatic ice dispenser had died long ago and the ice tray contained only white powder.

That left the horizontal freezer in which they'd put Fred's

body. Macy was not particularly squeamish nor was she superstitious, but the sight of her friend's headless corpse was upsetting. Even before she looked at it. She knew there were several ice packs in the horizontal, the kind you bought at Walgreen's and put on swollen ankles, because she'd put them there herself to deal with boys' ongoing bumps, trips and whoopsie-dos. The ice packs were down at the bottom beneath the pizzas taking up very little space.

She stared at the freezer noticing for the first time how much it resembled a coffin. Only white. But they had white coffins, didn't they? For children.

Well come on girl let's get it over with. "Ice, ice, baby," she muttered reaching for the handle. She heaved it upward and looked down. Thank God. Thank God the ice packs were beneath Fred's feet and not beneath his headless neck. Reaching far in she grabbed both ice packs, straightened up and slammed the lid down.

CHAPTER 23
The House

The Road Dogs snaked slowly through the quickening gloom until they came to where Milton's Hollow Road dead-ended at the County BB T-section. Wild Bill turned his bike around so that it was heading back into the hollow, got off and lit a hand-rolled cigarette. The other Road Dogs got off their bikes. Mad Dog lit up and Doc reignited his cigar.

"Fuck," Wild Bill said in a cloud of smoke. "We must have missed it. How come there ain't no gate entrances nor nothin' on that road?"

"It's there," Chainsaw said. "Maybe we can spot it going the other way."

Doc had seen a couple possibles but kept his mouth shut. Maybe if they could bullshit their way through the night without encountering Helmet Head everything would look different in the morning. They couldn't go back to the Klub—not once word got out about Fred. The place would be crawling with cops, possibly the Feebs or ATF or Homeland Security, always eager to sniff out MC gang activity.

Doc's kid Mandy was thirty now, the owner of her own pizzeria in some hoity-toity community out on Olympia across from Seattle. She was living with a fine young man who was working toward his veterinary degree while bouncing at a local nightclub. Come morning Doc had half a mind to light out for Seattle and to hell with Wild Bill and the Mad Dogs.

Curtis excepted, of course. They'd been friends before they'd been Mad Dogs. They weren't there to avenge Larry. They were there to have each other's backs.

He sidled up to Curtis. "Curtis. Let's go to Seattle tomorrow."

Curtis stared back down the way they'd come. It looked like a tunnel. "Sure," he said. The trip had turned into a goat fuck.

Mad Dog trucked over. "What are you two lovebirds cooing about now?"

Curtis lunged at him without warning. Mad Dog squeaked and took a little hop. Doc and Curtis laughed. Mad Dog sulked and turned away.

"Doc," Wild Bill said. "Maybe you oughta lead. You're good at that trackin' shit, that's what you always tell me."

"I never told you that, Bill," Doc replied patiently. "I was a medic. Curtis was a medic."

Mad Dog pounced. "Yeah, but you killed all them slants, that's what you keep tellin' us!"

"I said under duress that I had killed during wartime in self-defense. Now shut the fuck up before I jam my fist down your throat and rip out your heart."

Mad Dog made a suck me gesture with hands and bowed legs. Not for the first time Doc wondered if Mad Dog might be slightly retarded or autistic. Mad Dog seemed impervious to pain which would support certain types of autism. Doc wasn't sure how old Mad Dog was or if he even had parents. He'd been a pledge for two years. Either he had the patience of Job or he was too stupid to realize he was being stalled. More than once it had occurred to Doc that Mad Dog might be one of Wild Bill's bastards.

"Well what about you, Curtis?" Wild Bill said. "Your night vision's better'n mine anyway."

"I suppose you're gonna blame that on Nam, too," Curtis said.

"Whatever. You wanna lead or not?"

"I'll lead. I want to find that motherfucker as much as you."

Chainsaw returned from pissing in the woods.

"You better run a dick tick check," Doc said. Chainsaw gave him the finger.

They got on their bikes and once again snaked into the hollow this time with Curtis in the lead. Curtis had built his own chopper from an old Honda 750 four-cylinder sitting low in a stretched out frame, springer front end, softail rear. It was one sweet ride and probably the fastest bike in the bunch. With Doc riding flank Curtis entered the tunnel of trees at 25 mph.

They had gone perhaps two miles when Curtis abruptly signaled a stop. He kicked out the stand, got off his bike and walked to the right side of the road staring into the woods. He stepped into the ditch and up the other side, thrashing around in the underbrush. He turned around.

"Well this here's a road, looks like it's been concealed with cut branches." He reached down and started pulling the loose branches off the hard-packed earth. Mad Dog and Chainsaw joined him and soon they'd uncovered a dirt road going uphill into the forest. Doc came down with a flashlight, tried to see where the road led but it disappeared behind intervening growth. The road itself looked smooth and well-used although now it was a strip of mud.

"Move your ride," Wild Bill said maneuvering his hog. "I'm leading."

Curtis and Doc were happy to oblige. Bill duck-walked his bike down the slight incline into the ditch and up the other side followed by Chainsaw on his chop, Mad Dog on his Sportster, Doc on his Road King and Curtis on the modified 750. Curtis' bike was so low he had to scramble and push. All the bikes wound slowly through the forest up the winding path. The boys had to use their feet to keep the bikes upright at low speed in the mud. Their boots were caked with it.

Doc glanced to his right and thought he saw a gleam of metalflake red. Signaling to Curtis behind him, he stopped his bike and got off. The others rode on twenty feet and stopped.

Bill twisted in his seat. "What?" he yelled.

"There's something back here," Doc said drawing his revolver. He waded through the thigh-high grass, blackberry and alder until he could just make out what had caught his eye.

It was a full-face motorcycle helmet, an expensive model mounted on a crude wooden cross. Doc pushed forward but his legs encountered something hard and springy. He looked down. It was a wire hedge trim. Doc saw the other crosses and helmets.

"Jesus fucking Christ," Wild Bill said behind him, breath like an open wound. "Yeah, I'd say we found the fucker all right."

"We ain't found 'em yet," Doc observed quietly grasping the pistol and looking around. The burial plot was perhaps twenty by twenty and contained at least a dozen graves. Not all the wooden crosses were marked with helmets. Most held some other memento: a bandanna, a pair of wrap-around sunglasses, leather vests with patches.

Doc spotted the most recent addition a split second before Mad Dog.

"Holeeeee shit," Mad Dog said stepping over the barrier. "That's Larry's patch! Fuckin' Larry is buried right here!"

"No he ain't," Chainsaw said. "You heard the pig. He found Larry's headless body. What, the freak's gonna come back for the body so he can bury it?"

Mad Dog grabbed Larry's colors and held them up. "What are these doing here?"

"Maybe that's his head," Doc said.

"His head was in the helmet bag," Curtis said. "Listen, we can't stand around here jawing about whether to dig up Larry's head. Where's that road go, that's what I want to know."

"Curtis is right," Wild Bill said turning back to the bikes.

Fifty feet on they came to the house.

CHAPTER 24
WOTAN

An old two-story wood frame house with a listing porch that ran the length of the front. It might have been painted pale green once but now it was gray. The shutters and trim retained their forest green color. All the windows appeared intact and a light glowed softly from a first floor window toward the rear. Three listing wooden steps led up to the porch. At nine o'clock facing the front door a stone chimney anchored one end of the house.

The boys stopped at the bottom of the drive right before it veered toward the old barn, a hundred feet from the house. The barn was gray with double barn doors closed. It looked slightly out of whack as if the ground has shifted, like a Berni Wrightson drawing. It looked like it might topple in a strong breeze. A wrought iron weathercock shrieked intermittently in the wind.

"Well well well," Wild Bill said getting off his hog. "I do believe we've treed the fucker. Doc, you and Curtis come with me. Chainsaw, you and Mad Dog check out the barn."

"How come we have to check out the barn?" Mad Dog whined.

Wild Bill pointed at him. "Because you're a pussy. And pussies belong in the barn."

Doc and Curtis scoped the yard as they'd been trained to do. Doc noticed right away there were no cables to the house— no power lines, no telephone. No generator whine. What was the source of the lighting? He spotted ventilation for the septic tank that was often a rural home's only option.

The wooden stairs groaned in protest as Wild Bill stomped up to the deck announcing his presence without saying a word. Two old Adirondack chairs sat on the deck. A faded rubber mat said WELCOME. Wild Bill pulled back the screen door and hammered with four ounces of silver on the door.

"HEY MOTHERFUCKER! TIME TO PAY THE PIPER!"

Doc reached past him and tried the door handle. The door was unlocked. The boys poured in, two wide-bodies and a slim body. Immediately before them a set of Mayan steps led to the second floor. The living room was to their left. A hall led straight back to the kitchen whence the soft light glowed. All three stood in the vestibule momentarily silent, unnerved by the ease with which they'd entered.

The house smelled ancient save for a tendril of drool. Something delicious on the stove. Something involving garlic. Their stomachs rumbled. Dust, a faint air freshener whiff of the fifties, the residue of thousands of meals, dirty work boots tromping in and out, the perfume of a young girl's first prom, a faint odor of cat piss as subsequent owners commenced their long slide into oblivion.

Who knew by what circumstances the house stopped being a home and a working farm and became a derelict, a bum that squats in one place year after year? The bum's clothes were old but they were clean, frayed around the edges but still worn with dignity.

What had kept it safe from marauding teenagers and meth cooks? Why fear of course.

Kids knew. There were always places like this, surrounded by rumor and "dare-yas." Then they grew up and set aside childish things like spooks and haunts. Maybe not the bikers.

You couldn't find a more superstitious lot, their bikes festooned with good luck charms, St. Christopher Medals or bells. In their antinomian spirit bikers embraced the ugly and the profane, choosing skulls and bones as their good luck charms. The Grim Reaper, heavy metal, the Grateful Dead. Nazis.

Doc and Curtis had heard the Helmet Head rumors at Sturgis going back fifteen years—part of the dark canon of biker lore that got passed around after midnight. Like the crotch rocket rider who embedded himself in the back of a semi at 120 mph. The trucker drove seventy-five miles before he realized there was a dude hanging from his rear gate by the helmet. The squid broke every bone in his body. The picture of the boneless body embedded in the back of the truck circulated over the internet for months. It was still out there.

"What's that smell?" Wild Bill said.

It was a miracle he could still smell out of his abused proboscis. Bill and Curtis headed for the kitchen. Doc went into the living room and faced the dark fireplace in which ashes had piled. Above the mantle a stuffed boar's head glared down, tusks curling like Kaiser Wilhelm's mustache.

There were no wild boars in Southern Illinois.

A head model with a full bandanna face mask and leather skull cap rested next to three trophies, so oxidized the bronze plaques were unreadable. Doc picked one up and brought it close, standing next to the window to read the script.

PAN AM GOODWILL GAMES 1978
KENDO—FIRST PLACE JUNIORS
HELMUT VON MULVERSTEDT

There was a black and white photo of a tall young man in a kendo uniform, helmet under one arm, a handsome, serious face like that of some twenties matinee idol.

Great. The dude was some kind of sword master.

Doc picked up the cast iron fire poker and crouched as he'd learned to do in Nam. He and Curtis could crouch with the best of them. Crouch for hours. Doc poked around in the charcoal.

He fished out a cat's rib cage and what looked like the remains of a human hand. Something seemed to be written in thick letters on the back of the fireplace wall. It stood out even through multiple layers of soot, like one of those optical illusion moiré patterns that cleverly conceal some message.

Doc stood, grabbed a kitchen match off the mantle and lit it against the stone fireplace. He crouched and held the match up to the back.

WOTAN

Written with a black marker pen.

"Hey Doc," Curtis called from the kitchen. "Take a look at this shit."

"Yeah, just a second."

Straightening, Doc felt a sudden pain in his knees, put a hand on the mantle to steady himself. Getting old was a bitch. He carried a daily pill box. Seven little compartments filled with an assortment of gaily colored medications. Shit for his cholesterol, heart, kidneys and prostate. If he took the pills without food they upset his stomach. Come to think of it, he was starving and something savory emanated from the kitchen.

Doc walked back. The boys stood around the refrigerator which was plastered with clipped out news articles held in place with gay little magnets: Scotty dogs, daisies, bluebirds. Curtis pointed to a faded newspaper clip. Doc peeled it off.

VACATION ENDS IN TRAGEDY

June 22, 1987. Dr. Helmut Von Mulverstedt's dream of an American vacation ended in tragedy Thursday when he lost control of his car on Milton's Hollow Road, resulting in the deaths of his pregnant wife and two children. Von Mulverstedt himself was paralyzed from the neck down and remains in a coma at Our Lady of the Redeemer Hospital in Paducah. The accident was reported by a motorist at nine forty-five Monday night.

The story skipped to page A13. There was no other clip. It must have fallen down or been destroyed. Doc plucked another news clipping, this one about a headless biker found in the

Town of Dunn, 2002. Another in Lake Foster a few years later. The

latter clipping held a ketchup stain as if it had been pulled from the garbage.

A photo lay face down half under the fridge. Doc squatted and picked it up. It showed the tall, young, lean, blond father with his lovely young wife and two kids, about three and four, smiling in front of their rental SUV, about to embark on their grand American tour. The rental agency lay in the background. Doc stared hard at the photo.

He handed the photo to Wild Bill. "Who does that look like to you?"

Wild Bill brought the photo in, adjusting for focus. He pulled it back. "No shit!" he said. "How weird is that?"

Curtis took the photo from Wild Bill. "This ain't no coincidence."

Doc took the photo back and affixed it to the refrigerator with magnets. Helmet Head's wife was a dead ringer for Macy. Doc noticed a recipe taped to the freezer door. It was in German. Roast Bavarian boar.

"What's that smell?" Curtis said sniffing around like a bloodhound.

Wild Bill put his hand on the old gas stove. "Stove's on." He looked around, found a homey knitted hot pad in a floral pattern, opened the oven door and slid out the metal shelf holding a covered pot roast. The boys could hardly contain their hunger. Bill literally drooled. Their grumbling bellies competed with the thunder. Wild Bill used two hot pads to hoist the big ceramic-covered blue pot to the stove top and lifted the lid.

Larry's head had been roasting for an hour and the skin was peeling off in slices. It was a wrinkled coco as if browned in olive oil. The teeth had been removed and the mouth sewn shut. One mustard eye turned toward Doc like a hard-boiled egg.

CHAPTER 25
VALK

Chainsaw unlashed the Stihl from the back of his chop, slung it over his shoulder via leather strap and carried his long-barreled magnum in his right hand. Mad Dog held his nine out in front sideways like he'd seen in *Menace II Society*. He'd never killed anyone and he was twitchy as hell. Chainsaw knew it. They all knew it.

Chainsaw liked the risible and obstreperous punk. Mad Dog brought new blood to the group. He followed their orders no matter how disgusting or degrading. He offered his flesh as a canvas for every tattoo artist and body piercer that crossed his path. He had enough silver through his nose, tongue and eyebrow to back the Guatemalan National Bank.

Mad Dog lived to fuck with citizens and cops. He had no grand plan for life. He wanted to brawl, ball, drink and ride. He had "BORN TO RAISE HELL!" inked on his chest in 36 point Gothic. He had a skull with a snake winding through its eye on his left bicep. He had no more sense than a gerbil on acid.

Both Chainsaw's arms were covered with intricate, multi-colored Japanese-style illustrations of demons, samurai and geisha.

Chainsaw tried to remember when life was that simple. He'd joined the Marines at nineteen, served two tours of duty in Iraq and had one king hell bitch of a time returning to civilian life. Chainsaw had mad skills as a wrench and could operate heavy machinery but he could not seem to hold a job. His temper always got the best of him.

He couldn't stand stupidity, incompetence or condescension. No matter where he worked there was always some fucker who rubbed him the wrong way, often deliberately. Chainsaw did not seek out confrontation.

It sought him.

He was a beat down magnet. Part of it was the way he looked: Jason Statham's older brother. You'd think people would leave him alone. He was a perfect visual representation of what he actually was. Part of it was the way he spoke: heavy drawl. Part of it was the blue/black/orange/yellow ink up his arms. The Road Dogs were the closest thing he'd found to family. Chainsaw had worked briefly for a best-selling author, a household name, who maintained a fleet of three dozen classic and sports cars. Chainsaw maintained the fleet. He even helped whip the author's nineteen-year-old son into shape when the kid got into drugs. Saw took him for a little hike in the Rockies. Just Saw and the boy, ten days in the wilderness. The kid came back a man. The author was eternally grateful. He even dedicated a novel to Chainsaw. *The Lake Harmony Monster.*

But when Saw got the call he quit that job to be with his brothers.

The author's name was Carl Carruthers. His fictional hero Zach Moorehead represented LOCK, League of Conservationist Kooks, who sought to preserve endangered species. Carruthers took on Japanese whalers, African rhino poachers, even American Indians exercising their tribal rights to cull bald eagles.

Chainsaw tried to read one. He thought the whole thing was ridiculous, but Carruthers was extremely successful so he had to give him that. Carruthers lived in a 15,000 square foot French chateau with an enormous underground garage near Lake Geneva, WI. He also had twelve motorcycles including a Vincent Black Lightning, a Brough Superior, a Flying Merkel and two Excelsior-Hendersons, old school and new.

Saw preferred his Harley.

Chainsaw had been married for three months to a whore named Tiffany. The very thought of her name made him ill.

Tiffany. How could he have been so stupid? Well, drunk and stoned was more like it. Seemed like a good idea at the time. Back in the nineties, at the Golden Nugget in Las Vegas.

A pole dancer!

More like a goddamn hooker. Not that Chain had anything against hookers. They were some of the best fucks he'd ever had. But when he caught Tiffany fucking her ex-boyfriend, a bouncer at Griffin's on Fremont, he beat the dude unconscious and slapped Tiffany around like a handball until a neighbor heard the screaming and called the cops.

Bitch pressed charges and Saw spent six months in lock-up. Took him two more years to get rid of her.

Mad Dog stopped at the closed barn doors and shot Chainsaw a look. The doors slid sideways on rails. He needed direction. Chainsaw gripped his magnum in both hands, assuming a shooter's stance and nodded toward the door.

Mad Dog pulled on the left barn door which opened slowly with a horrendous shriek. Mad Dog pulled it all the way to the side and crept toward the entrance with his nine on his cheek. Chainsaw approached, grabbed the right door and walked it back. The interior was black as tar. Realizing he was framed against the evening light Chainsaw quickly stepped inside and to the right, back against the inside front wall.

Mad Dog copied Chainsaw. Mad Dog wanted to be Chainsaw. Wild Bill saw it and didn't like it. Wild Bill thought Mad Dog should want to be Wild Bill. Now they were both in the barn on either side of the door guns pointed at the middle. Something dark huddled in the center of the sawdust-covered floor between the stalls.

Chainsaw stumbled against a heavy tin. He felt behind him along the wall for a switch, found one. A single sixty watt bulb hanging at the end of a frayed fifteen foot cord cast a cold light on something low, black and spiky with the density of a small planet. Helmet Head's chop. Metal spikes protruded from the fork on either side of the massive front wheel. More spikes formed a Mohawk down the top of the tank. Chainsaw inadvertently shivered. He had an aversion to choppers that looked like ranks of Roman spears or shish kebab skewers. If your ride went down you didn't want it to stick you like a cocktail olive. It looked like some antediluvian monster left over from an earlier age. A mechanical megalodon or triceratops.

Mad Dog sucked in his breath. It sounded like air brakes. "That's his bike," he hissed in a stage whisper.

"No shit, Sherlock. But where's the big guy?" Saw looked down. A steel gas tank sat against the wall. Through an open stall door he saw a jumble of motorcycles and parts casually tossed like they were children's toys.

For a second he tensed and shifted, straining to see into every corner. The barn felt empty. Why would the dude hang out in the barn? He wouldn't. The barn was silent. No snort or pig squeal. No chicken squawk or field mice scurry. Even the animals knew.

The barn was waiting. Maybe it was waiting for them.

Mad Dog approached the bike stealthily like a man sneaking up on a sleeping dog. He vogued into a leaning A-frame two feet away.

"It's a Valk!" he hissed.

A Honda Valkyrie with a six-cylinder boxer engine.

At some level Chainsaw felt a deep relief. He had feared the bike was an infernal machine powered by the flames of hell. Chainsaw wasn't a religious person. He didn't much think about it. But he took it as a given there was a hell and he was probably going there. He was not a reflective man. But every now and then he weighed the good against the bad and found himself wanting.

Grinning, Mad Dog crept forward extending his left hand. He paused inches from the handlebar as if playing charade. Chainsaw held his breath, afraid to speak. Slowly, ever so slowly, Mad Dog stretched his left index finger and touched the handlebar, jerking back as if from a red hot stove.

Nothing happened.

Mad Dog did a little victory dance, going down on one knee to blow on his pistol barrel. He rose, jammed the gun in his pants, looked from Chainsaw to the bike with that country-wide shit-eating grin. He approached the bike shining his grill on Chainsaw. A redneck minstrel show.

Don't do it, Chainsaw thought but the words froze in his throat. He couldn't speak. Something had hold of his larynx and had shut it down, cut off the flow of power and free will. He could only watch in dread fascination like he was watching a theatrical production, once removed from reality.

What would Zach Moorehead do?

Mad Dog gripped the handlebars and swung his right leg over the bike, seating himself on the broad leather saddle. He turned toward Chainsaw arms stretched in bodaciousness. Top of the world, Ma!

A skull-shattering shriek filled the barn. The stall behind Mad Dog slammed open propelled by a size 16 boot as Helmet Head rushed forward with his samurai sword held aloft. Mad Dog didn't even have time to look. The sword arced out and around too fast for the eye to follow. Mad Dog's head fell to the sawdust-covered floor with a thump and rolled.

CHAPTER 26
GRANDPA

Doc grabbed the hot pads, slammed the lid on Larry's cooked head and shoved it to the back of the stove. He turned the oven off. The worst part was his stomach. It overruled his head. He salivated like a dog staring at a string of sausages. All their stomachs rumbled. They were almost ready to eat that head.

"Yeah," Curtis drawled. "I'm hungry, too."

"Jesus Chris," Bill said turning away.

"There's shit in the living room," Doc said. "Dude's a kendo expert."

Curtis shook his head sadly as if he'd known it all along. "Well fuck."

"Show me," Bill grunted.

Doc led them back into the living room, showed them the trophies and the photograph. Bill stared at the stuffed boar.

"What's a fucking Kraut swordsman doing here?"

"That clipping in the kitchen," Doc said. "He was on vacation."

"Y'know," Curtis said, "seems to me they left something out. Guy like this, he doesn't suddenly lose control of his car.

He was German! They take pride in their driving. They got the Autobahn and shit like that. Not like the drunk hillbillies around here. What if something forced him off the road?"

"Like what?" Wild Bill said. "A deer?"

"Like a bunch o' bikers," Curtis said.

Wild Bill and Curtis stared at one another.

"What club?" Wild Bill said.

"You know damned well what club."

Doc said, "What are you talking about, Curtis? When did the Dogs ever run anyone off the road?"

"When we was in Baja."

Doc and Curtis had been going to Baja since the eighties. It was a private thing, not for the others. Ed had been president then.

Curtis turned on a table lamp next to an old sprung sofa. The lamp cast a sickly yellow glow through the dust-covered shade illuminating a thrift store coffee table holding an empty bottle of peppermint schnapps and an inlaid wooden presentation box. There was no television, but an old upright Sylvania radio stood in one corner.

Doc hesitantly turned it on. He saw ancient vacuum bulbs glow to life behind the threadbare speaker screen, followed by white noise. Twisting the station dial only altered the pattern of noise. He switched it off. Where did it draw power? Had the power been restored? Doc doubted it. The storm wasn't over. No one was climbing power lines in this weather.

Yet the lamp lit. The house had power.

Doc sat on the sofa and reached for the presentation box. He opened it. Six silver commemorative coins nestled in red velvet. He picked one up.

Fassnacht Pharmaceutical, Collector's Club Commemorative Coin, 1980. The design showed a scientist in a lab coat holding a beaker to the sun. The other coins were similar, going through 1986. Doc turned the coin over. ***"Herrschaft der Natur durch Wissenschaft"* in Gothic script over a gleaming factory set amid a cornfield.**

They tried that, Doc thought. Doc's old man had fought in the Battle of the Bulge and died a few years ago aged 94. Doc slowly scanned the room with fresh eyes. The boar's head, the bones in the fireplace. An old black and white photograph in an elaborate gilt frame all but hidden in an unlit corner of the shabby room.

With a growing sense of trepidation and unreality he heaved himself out of the low sofa, banging his knee on the coffee table and crying out.

"Y'all right?" Curtis said.

"Just clumsy." Doc straightened up and walked over to the dingy corner, feeling every one of his sixty-plus years. Damn he needed some ibuprofen. He plucked the old photo from the wall. It was about four by six and showed a ramrod straight German soldier posing proudly, one hand on his dagger. In the background was a high brick wall topped with barely visible concertina wire. Judging by the size of the gate and the two soldiers in the background, it was about fifty feet behind the subject.

He wore the black uniform of the Waffen SS. Although it was too small to see, Doc was certain he wore the Death's Head symbol on his black officer's cap.

They heard the unearthly wail from the barn followed by six pops and the sound of a chainsaw.

CHAPTER 27
CHAINSAW

Chainsaw pulled the trigger when Mad Dog's head hit the floor and didn't stop until the long gun lay smoking and inert in his hands. Each percussion snapped a jolt up both arms but Saw was a trained shooter and automatically adjusted. He placed each shot in a cluster no larger than a dinner plate in the center of Helmet Head's chest, noting the tiny eruptions of black leather. He placed the sixth shot dead center on HH's visor. It kerranged off without leaving a mark.

Helmet Head stood immobile on the other side of the bike, sword at his side. He reminded Chainsaw of the robot in *The Day the Earth Stood Still*. For five seconds they stared at one another.

It was the longest five seconds of Chainsaw's life.

Casually, Helmet Head walked around the bike toward him. He was about twenty feet away. Chainsaw unlimbered his chainsaw unconsciously aping Helmet Head's *iaido*, the art of drawing the sword, striking the target, and returning the sword to its sheath in one smooth motion.

Chainsaw held the chainsaw down and yanked on the cord. It was wet from the rain. It sputtered. He yanked again, looking up like a trapped fox. Helmet Head paused, obviously waiting for Chainsaw to start the engine.

Gentlemen start your engines.

Chainsaw yanked three, four, five times and on the sixth the chainsaw sputtered into life. Saw gripped it ferociously in both hands circling away from the wall to give himself room. He'd been in knife fights. He expected to get cut. Helmet Head whipped his katana to a near vertical position over his head and lowered into a samurai stance. They danced the dance of death circling each other clockwise. Saw goosed the chainsaw, loving the surging revs, needing that shrieky highway sound to amp up.

Body armor Saw's ass. He'd see how that worked when Saw laid his Stihl against the freak's ankle or wrist. Only a crazy person engaged in knife fights. Saw was crazy. His arms and torso were covered with scars. He'd once taken out two Iraqi insurgents in the dark with his Sykes-Fairbairn. He'd lost it in a firefight in Mosul. He still missed that knife, more than most of the people he'd known.

Helmet Head darted forward, faking low and whipping the sword up and around in a downward parabola. Saw dipped and dodged right, meeting the sword with his spinning chain, eliciting a massive spark as the sword leapt back in the kendo master's hands.

Saw had expected the steel to shatter. It did not appear to even be marked, although it was difficult to tell in the gloom. Saw knew a Japanese American in the Marines who regaled him with tales of the samurai and their awesome hand-forged swords. Miyamoto Musashi, Zatoichi, Togishi. How Toshiro Mifune had trained for years to authentically represent samurai on film. How the steel was made, folded over and over back in on itself, often containing the blood of its future master, often tested by beheading.

The sword caught the light and for an instant Saw saw the elegant *hitatsura* temper line like oceanic waves. And suddenly, the Dogs were there, Wild Bill, Doc and Curtis rushed in the door guns drawn and blammo—froze as if they'd hit a force field, mesmerized by the incredible sight.

"Don't shoot!" Saw yelled.

Wild Bill brought his double-barreled .45 up and squeezed off four rounds with two pulls of his trigger. The air violently expanded and contracted. "Fuck that shit," he said.

The four slugs struck Helmet Head dead center and he staggered back, recovering his balance and turning his attention to Wild Bill. Although no face was visible there was no question at whom he was looking. His gaze hit you like a fire hose.

Chainsaw charged aiming low. Without looking Helmet Head struck sideways and down splanging the spinning blade away and sparking like a tiny falling star. Wild Bill found the can of gas at his feet, jammed his pistol in his belt, picked up the can and sloshed gas toward the monster. It fell short but soaked a broad stripe of sawdust.

Doc saw it all happen. "Curtis!" he yelled. "Let's get the fuck out!"

Wild Bill wheeled on him with pinpoint pupils. "You stand your ground, motherfucker!"

Saw saw his opportunity and charged screaming. Sword kissed saw. Sparks flashed to the ground. The sawdust ignited.

"Fuck!" Wild Bill bellowed and booked. Doc was right behind him. They paused panting some twenty feet from the entrance and looked back. The flames grew rapidly. The barn would be a conflagration within seconds. A series of muffled explosions from discarded bikes split the air. They froze with indecision.

Doc reacted first. "Come on! We've got to get Curtis!"

"Fuck Curtis!" Wild Bill roared. "He can take care of himself!"

An unearthly wail rose from the flames, from the earth itself. Doc barely had time to stagger backward out of its path before a blazing comet burst from the barn with the grotesque figure of a headless corpse pinned to the fork spikes. Doc fell to his knees. Every part of the bike including the rider and wheels was ablaze. The thing roared into the middle of the yard and braked severely on the drive spewing gravel and tossing Chainsaw's headless blazing corpse like a bag of trash. It catapulted into a tree and bounced off.

Putting one foot down Helmet Head executed an impossible tire-shredding U-turn and turned the spiked death machine toward Wild Bill. Bill ran for the house as fast as his fat ass could go.

Doc turned and headed back toward the blazing barn.

CHAPTER 28
BAD DECISIONS

Fagan was conked out on the sofa when she returned. Asleep he looked even younger with his close-cropped curly hair ending in a widow's peak. The emerging purple goose egg and some scrapes failed to conceal his chiseled good looks. The way he talked and carried himself said big time, not Podunk. Not for the first time she wondered what his story was. She had ways of making men talk.

He was a dash of Big City. He was her wake-up call. She had a window of opportunity to reclaim her life. She didn't need to hurt anyone to do it. Except for Bill. But Bill had burned through all his chances and his nine lives.

I'm not gonna take it—never have and never will.

Lightning flashed through the high side window and minutes later the rumble of thunder. The storm was hanging around. Carefully so as not to wake the cop she sat next to him and gazed down. Didn't work. His eyes opened and fixed on hers. They were hazel.

She placed the ice pad on his forehead as he reached for her, seizing her by the waist and drawing her down to him. The ice pad fell to the floor. One big spark. They climbed in around and over one another like wrestling mink and the clothes hit the floor. Fagan on top, Macy with her legs wrapped around his waist and just before he was about to come she whispered, "Go for it!"

The comment infuriated him. Why couldn't she just keep her mouth shut?

He pumped harder and harder in a frenzy as the thunder rolled slowly over them. He came with such a fury of anxiety and satisfaction he sobbed.

Afterwards they lay under an old Army blanket on the sofa snuggling to the thunder. Macy giggled with a mixture of self-satisfaction and embarrassment.

"Who are you, Pete? Where do you come from? Got any family?"

"Grew up in Fairchild, Oklahoma. My old man is a Rabbi. I was adopted. He and my mother still live in the same house. I did two years in the Army, one tour of duty in Iraq and when I got out I took the fed civil service exam. That didn't go anywhere, so I went back to Olathe Community College and majored in criminology. I applied for a job in Duke County, Nebraska and that's how I got started."

"How'd your parents feel about you going in the Army?"

"They thought I was nuts. I told them it was just something I felt I had to do. My dad is fairly religious—I attended Sunday school every week and I was confirmed. It's like bar-mitzvah lite. I got a set of golf clubs. I don't know why. I hate golf."

"How did your parents feel about the Army?"

"The Rabbi hated it. 'Jews aren't soldiers!' He had this thing about Jews being conscripted into the Czar's Army. I mean let it go already. That was over a hundred years ago. You'd think he'd been drafted himself!"

"Were you adopted from Jewish parents?"

"No way of telling unless you want to pay for a DNA test. Why?"

"'Cause you look Jewish."

"What, the hair and the nose, right?"

Macy giggled.

"Well listen—the Jews, God bless 'em. They're good people. But they're not soldiers, police or firemen."

"What about the Israelis? They seem pretty tough to me."

"Okay—fine. My point is, I don't feel like I have Jewish blood.

"I despise that image of Orthodox Jews with the curls, prophylactics and heavy wool coats. It just seems unmanly. I now know it isn't but when you're a kid image is everything. Didn't matter that I was adopted. My so-called peers picked on me all through school. Not complaining—it is what it is. I guess I've been unconsciously rebelling against my parents' expectations. What a shocker, huh?"

Macy ran her fingers through Fagan's curly chest hair. He wore a gold Star of David on a thin gold chain. She wondered if he'd start balding in a few years like most of the hairy guys she knew. Unlike Wild Bill, Fagan's stomach was as flat as Kansas.

"I guess I should have used a rubber, huh?"

"Don't worry. Ain't gonna happen. So tell the truth, officer. What are you doing down here? Burn some bridges did we?"

Fagan was silent for several seconds parsing his words. "I got my partner killed."

CHAPTER 29
ANGELA

Rayburn in Duke County, Nebraska, was a fast-growing community about eighty miles southwest of Lincoln. Flush with ethanol money, Duke County was eager to expand in the face of anticipated growth. In addition to tax revenues, the department had received a $900,000 grant from the Department of Homeland Security to beef up their force and equipment, including the purchase of a unique armored police vehicle from Carbon Motors.

Terrorists could conceivably target the Drake-Hayburn ethanol refinery.

The Sheriff's department went from three deputies to ten. Fagan was one of the new hires. Fresh off his stint with the military police at Camp Pendleton he was a poster boy for law enforcement recruitment. He had a BS from Nebraska State in criminology and was working on his Masters. He was the fifth new deputy hired. He started in May and by June he'd talked the department into buying him a Harley police bike which he used to enhance fattened county coffers. The Board of Selectmen singled him out for praise.

Weekend in June he caught a bad one. A biker lost control at a tight curve on County Trunk AA, left the road and hit one of the support wires for a power line, decapitating himself. Ten riders, five old ladies. The Mongrels: scrofulous, nasty and mad. The area was popular among bikers because of the Blue River Breaks. It was the only hilly country for hundreds of miles. Fagan was on the scene in six minutes, but by then numerous bikers and drivers had stopped to rubberneck and the road was a nightmare.

When a kid in Joe Rocket duds got off his crotch rocket and approached the corpse with a camera a Nomad shoved him savagely causing him to fall and strike his head on a rock. Fortunately, he was wearing a full-face Shoei helmet sparing him serious injury.

Fagan entered this scenario as the only law enforcement officer. The bike helped. He got off and went up to the hulking hirsute Nomad who'd shoved the squid. His name was "Ice Pick."

"I'm Officer Fagan. Is that your brother?"

Ice Pick was near tears, his huge ruddy face twisted in pain, beard bristling. "Yeah! Sorry Sam got outside on the turn and hit some gravel! Been riding with him for fourteen years, man! That motherfucker tried to take some fuckin' ghoul pictures!"

"All right, Ice Pick, it looks like he's okay. But we've got to make room for the ambulance and avoid other accidents. Could you and your brothers calmly and politely encourage these people to move on? And flag down any oncoming traffic?"

Ice Pick stared at him and reset his jaw. "Yeah. We can do that."

Fagan stuck out his gloved hand. They shook. "Calmly and politely, Ice Pick."

"Got it."

Fagan went over to the corpse sprawled chest down at the edge of a cornfield. The cut was nasty. White spinal bone poked out of red meat. Fagan looked around for the head, found it twenty feet into the corn.

After that he was the gang expert.

One day in early July Fagan sought refuge from the heat at Carl's Cafe, an old-fashioned diner out on Highway 78 near the fairgrounds surrounded by corn. Corn for the ethanol factory. Every motorhead and biker who ever lived hated ethanol with a passion reserved for the utter depths of bureaucratic stupidity. Ethanol could kill your engine. The higher the percentage, the more corrosion it caused. It drove up the price of food and did nothing to bring down the price of fuel. It was a crooked crony deal between the government and Drake-Hayburn.

The sun hammered mercilessly. Fagan pulled the heavy police bike around to the side and parked it in the shade of the building, gazing across the knee-high cornfield to the silver grain elevators in the distance, on the edge of town. He took off his helmet and placed it on the seat. He scratched his scalp furiously. He entered the air-conditioned diner, nodding to the other patrons, two old farmers and a traveling salesman.

Taking off his Psycho shades he sat on the red Naugahyde stool at the chrome and linoleum counter. He wore a tan, short-sleeved shirt with epaulets and khaki trou. His nine rode high on his hip. The fresh-faced brunette squared up in front of him like a pitcher.

"Hi! You must be one of the new cops."

"Pete Fagan, ma'am."

She pointed to the patch on her blouse. "I'm Angela. What can I get for you, officer?"

"Got any iced tea?"

"You betcha! Want a slice of pie with that?"

"No thank you, ma'am."

"Angela!"

She twirled, tossing her ponytail like a filly and drew an iced tea with unlikely flair. A couple of tourists stumbled in and took a booth at the window. Angela left to take their order. She was like a ruby-throated hummingbird, flitting from pistil to pot leaving a trail of light. Fagan caught one of the old-timers out of a corner of his eye winking at him.

Fagan pulled out his notepad and reviewed his notes from the morning meeting. Anthony Tuckett, who farmed corn and alfalfa on sixty-five acres north of town, had complained that kids on motocross bikes were ripping through his fields. There was a report of vandalized highway signs on 78 not far away. That would be his next loop. The interstate wasn't his problem.

He left that to the NHP. He had jurisdiction over all the county and city roads. Kids had been using Grange Road to drag-race since before Fagan was born and it had only gotten worse over time with the addition of the Fast and Furious crowd.

In the seventies and eighties they raced souped-up hot rods. Ford, Chevy, Dodge with drag slicks, blowers and traction bars. That began to change in the nineties with the influx of hot tuner imports. In Fagan's experience you were more likely to rip your head off in a Subaru than in a Ford. The auto manufacturers sold rigs like the Subaru WRX STI, the Honda Civic Si, and the Mitsubishi Lancer Evolution GSR.

The week before two kids got their Subaru up to 120 mph and hit an oak tree, tearing the car literally in half and killing both occupants instantly. Fagan's third assignment for the rest of the afternoon was to visit Rod's Tuners, a hop-up shop on 78 where the Fast and Furious met to modify their rides, bullshit and smoke dope. He wanted to meet the players, talk a little sense, ask for favors. Kids loved it when cops asked them for favors. Made them feel special and maybe, just maybe, a little more inclined to obey the law.

Angela brought the check.

It included her phone number.

The following week he stopped in again and asked if she was doing anything Saturday night.

"No I'm not," she said batting her eyes at him.

"Would you like to cruise Main, maybe see a movie?"

"I'd love to!"

"I have a car and a motorcycle. Which do you prefer?"

"Let's take the bike!"

She clung to him on the back of his Kawasaki like a lamprey. They watched *Spider-Man* and ended up in bed back at her place, an apartment building yclept Rolling Meadows. There was a lot of rolling but it wasn't in the meadows.

She had a bluebird tat on her left bicep and a rose on her rump. She was lush in shape and padding, the type of woman who tends to put on weight in later years. But right then she was perfect.

Like Fagan, Angela was older than she looked. She was thirty. She started putting out hooks in the third week.

"We should look for a place together."

In the aftermath of lovemaking Fagan said nothing. Angela felt the chill.

"What? Why not?"

"I didn't say anything."

"Come on, Pete. You didn't have to. I could feel you pulling away. Do you have other girlfriends?"

"Of course not."

"You like me, I like you. This way we'll be able to find each other at night!"

How did he explain to her his insane fear of commitment? He was thirty-two. He wasn't getting any younger. But hooking up with all that that entails? Fagan thought he knew women. He knew what it would entail.

When are we going to get married?

Let's have a baby!

Fagan's childhood alienation had psychologically damaged him. Much as the Rabbi and Esther tried to love him, he resisted and never felt he was part of the family. Always felt like he was a changeling dropped in their house by mistake. Like Harry Potter.

He didn't want kids! He'd seen them having meltdowns in the local IHOP. He'd picked them up for loitering, vandalism and worse. He'd seen one dysfunctional family after another which only reinforced his opinion that kids were too much work.

Kids were just nature's imperative to continue the species. They were not necessarily part of a rational life. Biology didn't care about love and faith. Biology only cared about getting on with the species.

They said becoming a parent changed a man but he was not eager to find out.

He never saw the happy families because they didn't phone the police.

It wasn't that he never wanted to get married. He just didn't want to get married in the foreseeable future.

"I think you should leave."

CHAPTER 30
TERRY

A week later Fagan was horny and called Angela up. They had a tacit agreement. She'd refrain from putting out the hooks and he would treat her as his girlfriend. This redounded to her favor in late September when she ran her Chevy Cobalt into a mail box after a night out with her gal pals drinking and dishing at the Crystal.

She called Fagan. "Pete, I ran into a fucking mail box."

It was on Winston Street not far from her apartment complex. The mailbox, belonging to Walt and Dotty Wilson's blond brick ranch house, was totaled. Walt stood in the doorway wearing a terry-cloth robe. It was eleven p.m.

The Cobalt had a minor scrape on the bumper. Angela remained behind the wheel, an open bottle of Coors on the seat next to her.

Fagan leaned in. "Are you all right?"

"Where's the fucking airbag?!"

Fagan made her get out of the car and checked her over. She seemed to be intact with a minor scrape on her forehead where it hit the steering wheel. She had not been wearing her seatbelt, a $99 fine.

Fagan reached in from the street side, pinched the beer bottle, and set it discreetly on the curb. He sat Angela down on the curb.

"Don't move."

He went up the flagstone path to talk to Wilson, who owned the local hardware store. Wilson was in his mid-fifties, roundish, with round glasses and a white comb-over that was better than Donald Trump's.

Everyone in town knew Fagan and Angela were an item.

Wilson came out on his front stoop. "Hello, Pete."

"Mr. Wilson. Very sorry about this. We'll get that mailbox repaired right away."

"Don't worry about it, Pete. I'm not going to press charges. It gave us quite a start, though. Dorothy and I were watching Leno when we heard a big bang. How's Miss Baxter?"

"She's fine, sir."

"I'll fix that mail box myself."

"At least let me pay for it."

"Don't worry about it, Pete. The town thinks you're doing a great job. You stopped those kids from using my walls as a canvas. I appreciate that."

Leaving his Crown Vic on the street Fagan drove Angela home in her Cobalt, depositing the empty beer bottle in a dumpster on the way into her building. He had intended to simply put her in bed and return for his cruiser but he ended staying a bit longer than he planned. It was twelve-thirty by the time he checked out for the day and headed home on his Kawasaki.

The next day the temperature fell twenty degrees and the rains came. Although Fagan had only been on the job five months, they teamed him with a newcomer named Terry Evans, a big farm boy from Des Moines who'd wrestled varsity for Iowa State.

Terry wanted to be a cop the first time he saw *NCIS: Miami* and *Law and Order*. He began hanging around cops in high school, joined the local Police Youth League, helped organize softball games and charity events and was generally looked at as a promising mascot.

He studied criminology while working nights as a security watchman for the Loomis Corporation, which put him through a basic training class covering everything from dealing with the public to the use of deadly force.

He did not carry a gun until he became a Duke County deputy. Fagan thought of Terry as a big, friendly Newfoundland. They worked together five days on, three days off through October. They put another officer on the bike. Fagan might have been a little zealous with the speeding tickets. He was disappointed but pleased he'd been tasked with showing Terry the ropes.

First couple of weeks piece of cake. Some fender benders, a deer collision, a couple of DUIs. Terry had a bluff and friendly manner backed up by a linebacker's body. The couple of times he had to assert himself he did so with finesse and restraint. He was Fagan's kind of cop.

The evening of November 15 was frigid and overcast with snow threatening. At nine thirty-five Fagan and Evans received a complaint about a domestic disturbance at 229 Fox Ave. in Browntown. That's what they called the southeast side where the Mexicans lived. And the Dominicans, Hondurans, and Guatemalans. But mostly Mexicans, who worked for Drake-Hayburn or the meat-packing plant.

Cops understood that some of these workers were undocumented or had overstayed their green cards, but most of the visitors were good Christian families, worked hard and stayed out of trouble. There had been no previous calls to 229 Fox Ave.

There had been no complaints.

The neighbors said it sounded like a war in there.

Snow started to fall in earnest as Fagan and Terry pulled up in front of 229 in their Crown Vic. The house was a shotgun shack, one of eight per block put up by Drake-Hayburn in the fifties to house migrant workers. The houses were uniformly shabby with listing steps and tilting shutters.

A couple teenagers stood in the street hovering over their BMX bikes as sounds of anger and destruction issued periodically from the house. Neighbors stood on their porches on either side. Fagan and Terry got out of the car. Fagan went up to a gangly boy underdressed in droopy pants with a pork-pie hat.

"You know who lives there?"

"Manny Galindez," the kid said.

"You know who all is in there?"

"Manny and his wife—I don't know her name, two kids, like five and six."

"Any guns in the house?"

The kid shook his head. "Never seen any but I don't hang with 'em."

Fagan thanked the kid and joined Terry on the narrow porch. He pounded on the door.

"Police! Please open the door!"

The caterwauling stopped. For a few seconds silence reigned. Fagan pounded and repeated his demand. They heard heavy footsteps approaching the door. It opened six inches. There was no chain. A mesomorphic Mexican peered out, blue Bible verse crawling up his neck in Spanish.

"Mr. Galindez, I'm Officer Fagan and this is Officer Evans. We have reports of a disturbance. Can we come in?"

The big man's tiny eyes looked fearfully from one to the other. "Is no disturbance. Nothing wrong here."

A woman moaned behind him. Terry went through the door followed by Fagan. Galindez' wife, if she was his wife, lay on the floor in the combo living/dining room with puffy eyes and purple bruises on her cheek and arm. The only decoration was a shrine to the Virgin of Guadalupe built around a garish plaster statue. It was surrounded by votary candles, coins, badges and bells not dissimilar to those favored by bikers, baseball cards, play money, a rosary. There were too many talismans to count. During the scuffle someone had knocked a pile of them across the threadbare carpet. A spray pattern of cards and junk. The ace of spades lay face up. None of the candles were burning or the house would have been in flames.

Terry turned Galindez around and cuffed him.

Fagan helped the woman to her feet. She was slight and dark with a Mayan nose and long glossy black hair. "Do you speak English, ma'am?"

"A little," she said.

"Let's go in the kitchen and you can tell me what happened."

Fagan led her by the elbow into the tiny kitchen and sat her down in one of the three mismatched chairs which looked like they'd been salvaged from the dump. Fagan remained standing. Everybody seemed to be cooperating so he didn't call for back-up. He took out his spiral pad and pen.

"What's your name, ma'am?"

"Juanita Galindez."

"You're Mrs. Galindez?"

"Yes. What about my children?"

"What children?"

"Esteban y Maria. They ran out the back when he hit me."

"Has he hit you before?"

Mrs. Galindez stared at the floor. "Please find my children. They must be all right." She fell to her knees and clutched his pants. "Please!" she sobbed.

Protocol demanded that neither party be left alone during a domestic dispute. There were good reasons for this but Fagan made a judgment call. Juanita seemed like a defeated woman, only her love for her children keeping her alive.

"You stay right here, understand?"

She nodded gratefully with a hint of a smile.

Fagan left the kitchen, glanced in the living room where Terry had Galindez seated on the sofa and was talking into his collar phone. Fagan went down the hall—there were two tiny bedrooms and a tiny bathroom. Neither child was in any of the rooms. Fagan went straight out the back porch, now covered with a half inch of freshly fallen snow. He looked around the shabby yard. There was a pit bull in a wire enclosure. He made a mental note to send animal control.

Child-sized footprints led away at an angle, partially obscured by the falling snow.

The scream cut the night like a razor. Two screams—a man's bellow of abject pain and a woman's soprano ululating madness from a vision no human can endure. Fagan rushed back into the house drawing his gun.

He stopped at the entrance to the front room. Juanita sat

next to her man, still sullen, still cuffed, consoling him and weeping.

Terry Evans lay on the floor face down with an enormous butcher knife sticking out of his back.

CHAPTER 31
WILD BILL RETURNS

They put me on paid leave. I saw the handwriting on the wall and resigned. I must have applied to sixty jurisdictions across the country. Bullard County was the only one that would have me."

Macy didn't know what to say so she said nothing. She thought about telling Fagan about Shane. It rose like a sounding whale stopping just beneath the surface. No. He didn't have the right to know. Not yet. Maybe not ever. For the thousandth time she wondered if she was crazy.

As a nursing student Macy had studied psychology, delved more deeply into it on her own. She devoured the classic texts like *The Mask of Sanity* and *Human Psychology*, compulsively watched *Dr. Phil*, *Addicted* and their endless ilk knowing that this was not "reality," as advertised in the listings, but show biz. Ginned up conflict to entertain the squares. The quirk of the week club: *Hoarders*, *Dance Moms*, *Big Bitch Texas*, *Bridezillas*. She couldn't get enough. Watched it in the bar when she was the only one there. Rattled off a list of diagnosis: borderline personality disorder. Schizophrenic. Extreme narcissism. A douchebag. A conniving cunt.

Macy used to think she knew how to size people up. That was before she met Bill. Obviously she didn't know shit. Still, she had a sense that Fagan was a man of honor, whatever the hell that meant. He'd already had his ass kicked going to her defense. And he was a cop. They were supposed to be men of character, although experience taught her they often were not. She knew outlaw bikers with greater character. Doc and Curtis came to mind.

Wherever bikers gathered they traded stories of cop perfidy. This is what happens, she thought, when you choose an antinomian path. If you set yourself outside the law of course you'll see the law as the enemy. On the other hand Macy had personally witnessed enough police bad behavior to know there were plenty of bad cops out there.

Lady cops were often the worst, probably because they carried chips on their shoulders and thought they had more to prove. A lady cop stopped Macy once for weaving all over the road. She was a light skinned black woman with laser scars on her buff arms from tat removal. She thought she smelled alcohol on Macy's breath, threw her to the ground and cuffed her without warning. They never did a breathalyzer or took a blood sample. Macy tried to file a complaint. A judge dismissed the charges. Wild Bill wanted to bushwhack the cop but Macy put the brakes on that.

She'd thought about being a cop for five seconds once, right after she spent ten minutes wondering whether she should join the Army.

The problem, she realized, was not knowing what she wanted in life. What did Macy want? Was it the marriage, the kid, the ranch house in the suburbs? Did she still want to be a nurse or had all the compassion dried up and blow away? No idea. The one thing she knew—she was going to keep this baby.

She became aware of the cop's beating heart against her ear.

"I'm sorry," she said.

"Not your fault."

"It's funny how the choices you make, you don't think anything about at the time, how they come back and affect your life."

"Yeah," Fagan said, shifting toward her to ease his arm. "Like stepping on a garden rake."

"But you weren't a motorcycle cop before."

"No," Fagan said. "But I was always a biker. Got my first bike when I was fourteen. I ride a Yamaha in my spare time."

"That thing."

"Helmet Head."

"I've heard about him."

"Where?"

"Sturgis, two years ago. We were partying with the Outlaws. Said that's how one of their guys bought it. Wild Bill tore him a new asshole."

"All these years," Fagan said, "the story's been out there."

"What if it comes back?"

Fagan disentangled himself and sat up. "We won't be here. Soon as it's clear we're leaving. We can take Fred's bike. We'll walk if we have to."

"Can't you hotwire the truck?"

Fagan grinned and put his pants on. "That's a big myth that every cop knows how to hotwire a car. I'm sure Wild Bill knows."

Macy sat up and put on her clothes. The wind howled. Thunder rumbled from afar. A faint whine intruded. At first Macy thought it was a tornado siren but as it waxed she recognized the distinctive rumble.

"That's Bill's bike."

CHAPTER 32
THE LIMBO ROCK

Macy was first out the door because Fagan stopped to put on his shoes and strap on his gun belt. As soon as he followed and saw the glow he knew he'd made another bad decision. He ran up to her, seized her by the shoulders and turned her away.

"Go back inside! Don't look!"

Macy twisted free of his grasp and ran a few steps. She stopped and stared in consternation at the fast approaching fireball. Bike and rider fused together by the flickering blue/green flames the wheeled comet accelerated as it entered the parking lot. Macy stood frozen. Fagan wrapped his arm around her waist and pulled her back out of the way as the monstrosity blazed by so hot it singed Macy's hair.

The rider and bike had become a single encrusted organism. In the split instant as it passed and just before it slammed into the side of the bar Fagan saw that the rider had no head.

A half ton of flaming bike and rider slammed into the side of the bar with a deafening report. Fagan sprinted for the bar, leapt the steps in a single bound and ran into the kitchen where he'd spotted a fire extinguisher. He ran back outside to find

Macy sitting on the ground, arms around her knees staring at the charred remains blistering the siding. It looked like the scene of a jet fighter crash. Fagan stepped up with the fire extinguisher and within seconds had put it out.

When he looked back Macy was quietly sobbing. He dropped the extinguisher, helped her to her feet and led her back into the bar where he sat her down on the sofa and covered her with the blanket.

"Stay here," he said. "I'll be right back."

"It's coming back," she sobbed. "It's going to kill us. It's going to kill my baby."

Fagan sat and put his arm around her. "It's not coming back."

Well that's another great career decision you've made, isn't it? Sleeping with a suspect/witness/person of interest was always a great idea on the cop shows—in real life not so much. Now what was he supposed to do? Stay and comfort her like a lover or perform his duties like an officer of the law?

Love her? He'd just met her! Sure he found her attractive and felt sorry for her. He liked the way she talked, too, but he was on the job! Their life together stretched before him, an hallucination flickering in blue/green flame.

"It's coming back and it's going to kill us," she blubbered into his chest.

Fagan disentangled himself and stood. "No it's not. It's not some mythological creature. It's just a big man with a lot of body armor." He tested his radio again. Nothing.

"Stay right there." He headed for the front door. The bike's impact had knocked glasses off tables and the custom steins off their shelf. They lay shattered in a field perpendicular to the bar.

Distasteful though it was Fagan had to make sure it was Wild Bill's body glued to the handlebars and seat. He went outside, down the steps and around to the side of the bar where the reeking mess had left a broad scorch. Smoke curled from the remains, the smell of gasoline, burning rubber and human flesh.

Using a pen light, Fagan approached with gloves on. The bike lay on its side, the body sprawled back but still connected. Fagan spotted the pocket chain and pulled Wild Bill's fat Harley wallet out from under him. It would have to do for now although later they would take fingerprints if they could.

Fagan wondered how the device had been kept upright and rolling without a head. He shined his pocket light on the black neck stump and that's where he found the implant.

It was a circuit board no larger than pack of cigarettes with a series of microchips and tiny gaily colored cylinders like you'd find in any radio-controlled toy airplane. It lay flat across the severed top of the spine with wires sinking into the neck. Two AAA batteries lay in tandem.

Fagan thought about taking it out and bagging it but who knew who deep it was sunk or to what else it was connected. Better leave it to the tech guys. One thing he knew. Helmet Head was not just a big guy in body armor. Whoever had engineered this infernal device was some kind of criminal genius. Fagan was a reasonably well-informed guy. He cruised the net and subscribed to the *Wall Street Journal* and *Scientific American*. This was zombie future thriller shit. Nobody was even talking about animating headless corpses.

He flashed on a dark vision: dozens of headless corpses in coveralls carrying pickaxes marching into a mine. Yo-ho. Yo-ho. It's off to work they go. Headless soldiers marching off to battle. Headless police. Headless Occupiers.

Der Golem. The murderous clay monolith of Jewish legend.

Fagan touched the star around his neck.

The implant changed everything. It was now a federal matter, and possibly Homeland Security. The technology had frightening implications for terrorism. Which begged the question, how could some freak recluse living in the backwoods of Southern Illinois have developed this shit?

Fagan examined the body more carefully. The pistol was gone. Nor did Wild Bill appear to be carrying any other weapons. Fagan felt a lump in Wild Bill's black leather vest, ripped it up from his body with a disturbing sound, fished around in an inside pocket and drew forth a black-velvet jewelry box. He opened it.

A one karat brilliant-cut diamond on a gold ring.

It hit Fagan like a jackhammer to the gut.

He thought about pocketing the diamond. It would go a

long way toward child support.

Won't you do the Limbo Rock?

How low can you go?

Sighing, he replaced the jewelry box in Wild Bill's pocket. Let the tech boys figure it out.

He thought he heard a muffled shout from the rear of the bar. Thunder rumbled, closer this time like a bully making another pass. Drawing his pistol Fagan approached the back parking lot in time to see the leaves moving as something big disappeared into the forest.

CHAPTER 33
JUST ONE SMOKE

Macy huddled on the sofa beneath the blanket thinking, *What have I done? What have I done?* Her world had changed in an instant.

Wild Bill was gone. She searched in vain within herself for some small sign of regret but all she felt was an overwhelming relief. It was as if a throbbing headache that had troubled her forever, which she refused to acknowledge, had suddenly disappeared.

Her euphoria lasted about two seconds before she returned to what she'd just witnessed and the reality of her situation. She was no longer fighting for herself. She was fighting for the baby.

Does that make me a bad person, she thought. Glad because the father was dead?

No.

Was it better for the child to grow up without a father?

Not necessarily.

She had a replacement all lined up and she asked herself, not for the first time, had she deliberately set out to seduce Officer Fagan in hopes he would take care of Wild Bill? Was that who she was?

Tears filled her eyes. She did not want to be a conniving bitch! She'd never been one to trade on her looks. She was a tomboy, someone who could take a joke, one of the guys. The other Road Dogs had all treated her with respect—even Mad Dog. She felt lost and alone and that made her desperate. Desperation made people do crazy things.

She'd only had five lovers in her entire life. She'd lost her virginity to Shane but the first guy to whom she gave it up was her boyfriend Jack in the back seat of his parents' '68 Chrysler. Their affair did not survive the following summer when Jack decamped to D.C. to serve as a Senate aid.

There were a couple guys in college, nothing serious, and then Bill.

It wasn't like she was Paris Hilton!

She knew all about the biological stupidities that led women to the wrong men. Deep voices, a hairy head, well-hung. Nature didn't give a shit about lasting marriages or mutual love and respect. Nature's only interest was propagation of the species. She knew what men were like. It had been so easy to seduce Officer Fagan. No wonder so many women preferred to make a living off their backs. Sure as hell beat nursing school if you liked that sort of thing. She giggled.

She thought briefly of getting on Fred's bike and getting the hell out of there. She knew how to ride—even had her own bike, if it was still in one piece, back at the trailer park. She doubted she'd make it far. She knew what these roads were like after a wind storm. There'd be trees and limbs all over. She looked at her watch. It had only been three hours since the cop showed up. It seemed like a week.

God she wanted a smoke. Hadn't had one since she took the test, a week ago. Before that she'd gone through a pack a day. Big whoop. Twenty-one cigarettes. She didn't drink. She no longer did cocaine or meth. What else could they ask? One fucking cigarette wasn't going to kill the baby. Considering what kind of day it had been she'd be well within her rights to upend the death's head corn liquor.

Just one. One lousy cigarette. She sat up on the sofa and scanned the table tops. She got up and shifted through the butts in the ashtray. Those fools smoked a cigarette until their fingers burned. What was she, some junkie sifting through detritus for a fix?

Well yes. She giggled again. What a day! And it wasn't over yet.

Fred smoked. Fred had cigarettes. She knew for a fact he had pack in his breast pocket. Maybe he had more in his room. She got up, grabbed a flashlight from behind the bar and went into Fred's room. She felt funny like she didn't belong. She'd only been in it a couple of times at Fred's request, when he sent her after something.

The room gave her the willies. A cursory search revealed no cigs. She had to go for the cigs in his breast pocket.

No biggie. She'd already been back there once. Fred was just frozen meat. He wouldn't begrudge her a cigarette. He never had. He'd been a good friend, a father figure although he wanted to jump her, she could tell. But Fred had always behaved himself and treated her decently, letting her stay when she couldn't get home. Loaning her money when she was short.

She felt a sob about to break surface and thought this is what it's like to go crazy. Laughing and sobbing, loathing and loving.

All right. Enough. Straighten up, woman! Get the cig.

She pushed open the door to the warehouse. The only light was what filtered through a single grimy window high up on the wall, the occasional flicker of distant lightning. Reflexively she looked around as she always had, entering the family basement. Shane could be anywhere. Behind the stacked liquor boxes or wedged between the furnace and the wall.

But Shane was gone. AWOL with no forwarding address. He had no idea if she were even alive, let alone where she was. Shane was not the problem. She had to get Shane out of her head, for the sake of the child.

She shook herself and made a gargling noise with her tongue, literally purging herself of fear.

She went up to the freezer, seized the handle and lifted the lid.

Ice cold fingers closed around her wrist like handcuffs.

CHAPTER 34
THE TRUCK

Fagan ran to the edge of the forest with his gun drawn but by then it was too late. The murk had swallowed it up, whatever it was. Maybe a bear. They said there were bears but he'd yet to see one. Black and brown bears, generally quite timid. Fagan turned and headed back to the club. He glanced at the rear and noticed that the door to the warehouse was open an inch. He was certain that he and Curtis had left it latched when they'd come through.

Pistol in hand he entered through the back door, standing just inside to let his eyes adjust to the diminished light. The horizontal freezer door was open. Fagan approached with gun half-raised and looked inside. Fred's corpse was gone.

With growing trepidation Fagan rushed through the kitchen into the club.

"Macy!" He whirled in the middle of the floor looking for her. Where could she have gone? He looked again more carefully. He checked the pile of blankets on the sofa and the two restrooms.

The enormity of what just happened smacked him like a Mack truck.

The thing had Macy.

If it could program Wild Bill's headless body to ride his bike into the side of the bar it could program Fred's corpse to grab her and run. But how had it managed to sneak in the back and wire up Fred without anyone knowing?

How had it managed any of its astonishing feats?

Was it even human?

Since WW II the Nazis had become the gold standard in evil. Never mind that crimes committed by Stalin, Mao and Pol Pot beggared those of the Nazis. Maybe it was the uniforms and the mystic mumbo-jumbo, Hitler's astrologer, his phrenologist and fascination with dark arts. The Spear of Destiny, *Raiders of the Lost Ark*, *The Boys From Brazil*. Had there ever been a greater stab at heinous immortality?

The Rabbi would simply say, "Hitler was an evil man."

Even as a young boy Fagan sensed it would be inappropriate to ask his father about the experiments, the gas chambers and more outré elements of the Nazi war machine.

The Rabbi didn't even like discussing *Der Golem*. "It's a fairy tale, Petey. Like *Frankenstein*."

The one thing Fagan remembered about *Der Golem* was how to get rid of it. Erase the sigil on its forehead. Fagan had wrestled with this as a child. As Der Golem was made of bone-crushing clay, how did you erase something inscribed in its granite-like forehead? Jackhammer? Dynamite? To do so you would have to be in the Golem's grip. Perhaps that was the point. The destruction of the Golem required blood sacrifice.

Fagan remembered an old VHS he found at a garage sale: *They Saved Hitler's Brain*. He bought it as a joke and never watched it. One girlfriend asked how he could even have such a thing on display in his man cave. He'd never thought about it much. All that business with the Jews in Germany during WW II seemed so distant. He couldn't relate despite his father's best efforts to inculcate in him a sense of grievance. Whether he had actual Jewish blood or not was immaterial.

Fagan had never identified with victims and too often Jews were victims. That was one reason he resisted the Rabbi's efforts so fiercely. None of the boys he knew admired scholars, Jewish or not. They admired fighters and athletes. Being blessed with a decent frame Fagan went that way. In his senior year he grew two inches. Coaches took a newfound interest in him. He excelled at track and basketball, was on his high school varsity, his name on the trophies in the front hall.

All in his senior year, like a late-blooming cactus.

"Petey," his father told him. "It's nice you're good with sports but you should also cultivate a life of the mind and of the spirit!"

Later, Pops. Got a hot date.

A brilliant flash briefly illuminated the bar through its slot window followed almost instantly by a 120 decibel crack. Fagan snapped his hands to his ears. He had to find Macy before that thing killed her. But how? He didn't know where to start. And how would he get there? Maybe that old motorcycle in the shed.

Fagan went behind the bar where they'd replaced Fred's shotgun. His feet crunched on broken porcelain from the steins. He looked down. A steel key lay near the toe of his boot. He reached down and picked it up. It bore the Ford logo.

Snatching up a box of Remington .12 gauge, Fagan strode back through the storeroom, out the back to the truck parked next to the shed. Fagan guessed its year as '78 or '79, but it appeared well maintained and he knew from experience old Ford trucks could go for hundreds of thousands of miles. He prayed that it would start.

Looking up, he saw an orange glow reflecting off the underside of low-hanging clouds and knew that Helmet Head would not be hard to find after all.

CHAPTER 35

WAKING UP IN A STRANGE BED

S he was a little girl hiding from Shane. Shane didn't want to just stick boogers in her hair. He wanted to stick his dick up her pussy. His words. She barely understood the first time he explained. Now she was thirteen and running for her life. The woods behind the house went down to a stream. Across the stream was a quarter mile of empty fields until the next house. They lived in an old farm rental outside town while Dad looked for work and Mom drank.

Her younger brother Brent stayed in his room in the basement playing with computers.

Shane had nailed her twice. She bled, and had to hide it from her folks. He threatened to kill her if she ever told. At thirteen she was a stick figure, a rag doll. Tiny tits and a boy's ass. At seventeen, Shane was pumped and primed. He lifted weights in the school gym after school, a fact that his counselors noted with irony as he often skipped classes.

Shane was already in trouble for "inappropriate touching" at school events. His hormones were out of control. He should have gone into the Army right then. All he thought about was pussy. Pussy pussy pussy. She could hear him at night jacking off in his room. She found his porn stash and ran in disgust. Shane was extremely good looking. He took after his mother.

When Macy tried to tell Bernice what was going on, she went into total denial and threatened to send Macy to a facility for disturbed children. Not her Shane. Not the star of the basketball court and the football field.

So here she was hiding in the woods, mosquitoes dining on her neck like it was a Country Buffet, and Shane swooping through the bushes singing, "Where *arrrrrre* you, Macy? Come out, come out wherever you are!"

She wished she had a bow and arrow. Drill that fucker right through the heart. What kind of brother rapes his own little sister? Since her parents seemed to side with Shane she felt she had no recourse except to run away from home. She'd already started packing and saving money. She had a friend who said there were youth shelters in Omaha that would take her in. She would find a lawyer and seek to be emancipated.

She was too little and too young to get a job.

She hadn't known about Child Protective Services. It never occurred to her to go to the police or her school counselor. These weren't things you talked about if you were a thirteen year old girl. At school she was shy, a loner, a target for bullies. They made fun of her goth urges, her shyness. Like chickens jabbing at a spot of blood.

She huddled in a copse of alder a couple feet from the stream listening to Shane thrashing around. A green snake slithered over her shoe. She almost cried out.

The woods went away. She stared uncomprehending at an old plaster ceiling, cheap light fixture in the middle, pile of dead insects gathered at the bottom of the globe, plaster trickling down from a couple of holes. She was lying down, on her back. She tried to get up. She could hardly move. A wave of nausea rolled through her. Oh God she did not want to throw up. She'd been doing that a lot lately. It was as if she were at the bottom of the Marianas Trench with 20,000 feet of seawater holding her down.

It took her a second to realize she'd been drugged. She knew that feeling all too well. Well they didn't know Macy.

What was she doing here? How did she get here?

Then she remembered Fred's headless corpse seizing her wrist and rising from the freezer like some kind of fucking vampire only instead of a head he had a little circuit board sticking straight up with a tiny camera on the top.

Fred's grip was like steel. She tried to scream but Fred struck her in the jaw with a brick-like fist knocking her out. That was the last thing she remembered.

Macy shook with revulsion and her body responded. The old bed squeaked in protest. Good! Let her memory get her motor running. She had years of experience fighting her way out of drugged stupors. Like that time they got a call at seven in the morning that the cops were on their way.

Okay, kid. Let's start with the right leg. Just the right leg. Tentatively she tried raising her right leg. It went up a couple inches and collapsed.

Come on that's no good! Is this the little girl who ran through the woods for miles and miles? Who rode her own chopper? Who got Wild Bill out of bed at seven a.m. after an epic 72-hour bender? And out the back door?

She tried again and this time succeeded in moving her buttocks close enough to the edge that her leg flopped over. It seemed to take forever fighting through Jell-O to get to a sitting position. What the fuck. She was wearing a red dress. Someone had undressed her and put her in this dress.

She sat and listened to her heart beat. She looked up. An old dresser with a stand-up photograph on top. The closet's cheap accordion door was shut. Putting one hand on the newel post Macy swayed to her feet. It was three feet to the bureau, a yawning gulf. She had to see that picture. Letting go the newel post she stumbled forward and caught herself on the top of the dresser nearly pulling it down on top of her.

The photo fell on its face. Holding on with one hand she picked the photo up and turned it over. Four by eight, faded color, possibly a Polaroid of the smiling family, tall, good-looking father, svelte blond mother, the two happy kids.

The mother's red dress. The sleeves came to just over the elbow with a discreetly plunging neckline. Macy looked at her arm. She was wearing the same dress. It felt old and smelled faintly of jasmine and mothballs.

Where was this place? What was she doing here? The room did not look like it belonged to a woman. The walls were bare, the furnishings minimalist. It was monk-like. One hand against the wall for support she went to the closet, the effects of the drug receding with every step.

She seized the plastic handle and compressed the door to the side. For a moment she stood there uncomprehending. She began to shake her head. The closet contained four sets of complete black leathers. Above each on the hat shelf was a full-face black helmet with a heavily tinted shield.

A quartet of monsters.

It took Macy a second to realize they were just outfits. Gasping, she fell back on the bed.

The front door opened and slammed shut.

CHAPTER 36
LONE SURVIVOR

The seat squealed like a stuck pig as Fagan shoved it back. He doubted Fred had let anyone drive his truck. Fagan set the shotgun and pistol on the seat next to him. The old Ford started on the first turn of the key. The interior was spotless. It smelled of dust and age. Fuzzy dice hung from the rearview and there was four on the floor. The shift knob was a giant red plastic die. The steering wheel sported a necker knob with a sixties-era nude. Shifting into first gear, Fagan pulled away from the shack hearing empty beer bottles roll and clink against each other in the bed. He drove around the club and onto the state road heading east toward the glow in the sky. The old truck accelerated smoothly up to fifty, which was as fast as Fagan dared push it in the gloom and storm. Eight miles on he came to the turnoff to Milton's Hollow. Several times he steered around broken branches lying in the road. Soon he was deep in Milton's Hollow, the forest gloom accelerated by nightfall. His headlights disappeared ten feet in front of the truck.

Fagan slowed way down. He came around a tight curve and the lights briefly picked up a mass of fur and muscle—a coyote dragging something out of the woods on one side and crossing over. It looked like a human arm.

Around another corner an ash tree lay across the road. Fagan thought about plowing through but the tree looked a little too big. Leaving the engine running and lights on he got out of the truck and examined the obstacle. A couple swift cuts with a chainsaw would do it. Fagan looked in the back of the truck. An old lawn chair next to a cooler. Fred liked to sit in the back summer evenings drinking and stargazing.

There was a galvanized tool box stretching the width just behind the cab. It was unlatched. He opened it and found numerous tools including a long-handled ax. It would have to do.

Stripped to his khaki t-shirt Fagan swung the ax. The wood's freshness made it hard work and the sound of the ax striking the tree struck Fagan as somehow obscene. Every swing of the ax caused his ribs to shriek in protest, other bruises adding to a bohemian rhapsody of pain. Pausing, Fagan looked up and saw red eyes peering at him from the forest.

Strange behavior for a coyote or a wolf. Fagan didn't care. Part of him actually hoped that something would lunge at him so he could bury the ax in its skull. Nevertheless, he went back to the truck and jammed his nine in his belt while he resumed his work. He chopped the trunk into three sections and laboriously dragged them to the side of the road.

By the time he finished he was drenched in sweat. He got back in the truck and drove through the rubble keeping an eye on the glow in the sky. It disappeared as he hit the bottom of a dense coulee, reappeared as he crested. He could smell burning wood, gas and hay through the open window. Thank God for the storms—at least the danger of forest fire was minimal.

He saw the crushed weeds, the road to the burning barn and took it, the old pick-up jouncing up and down on its springs. Lightning flickered, gleamed metallic red off one of the motorcycle helmets in the little cemetery. Fagan paused long enough to take it in, realized he was near the place Larry died. No time to investigate. Macy's life was in danger.

A hundred yards on he came to the yard. The Dogs' bikes

lay around like scattered toys. The barn was gone—collapsed in on itself, a bed of coal, leaving the blackened remains of a Caterpillar compact track and loader and the blackened bones of a jumble of bikes. A few overhanging limbs smoked but the woods were too wet to catch fire.

Fagan looked at the old farmhouse. He'd ridden past once or twice and had never known it was there. In the barn's dying flames and the flicker of lightning it looked like a listing pile of timber inhabited by vermin. The roof was absurdly steep as if it had originally been intended for a mountain climate. The chimney kinked like Fred's leg.

There ... was no sign of the creature's motorcycle.

A motion drew Fagan's attention back to the barn. A Kevlar-clad arm swept the air. A mound turned into a man. Slowly Doc sat up. Fagan ran to him.

"Doc! What the hell happened? Where's Macy?"

"Don't know. I was out to lunch. We found him. Fucker chopped off Mad Dog's head, barbecued Chainsaw, I don't know what happened to Wild Bill. Curtis got caught in the fire. I tried to save him...."

Doc ran out of breath and spasm coughed. Fagan could see Doc's jacket and beard were scorched, eyebrows singed, burns on his face, tears on his hands. The coughs came in choppy waves like an angry sea. Gradually they died down.

"Are you okay?"

"I'll live. Saw had a go at him before the fucker got 'im. That chainsaw was no match for his sword." Doc coughed spasmodically. "You wanna grab my kit and water bottle? It's in my left bag." Doc broke into another paroxysm of coughing.

Fagan gripped Doc's wrist. "Macy. It took her."

Doc shrugged. "I don't know anything about that, son. I only just now come around. But she might be in the house. We found Larry's head in the oven."

"Jesus."

Fagan saw something in Doc's eyes. "What?"

"There's a photo in the living room of some Nazi standing in front of a concentration camp."

"Great," Fagan said. He ran to Doc's bike lying on its side, ripped open the saddlebag and found the medical kit in a black leather zip-bag. He popped it open and put in a sealed plastic

water bottle and tossed it to Doc from ten feet. Doc snagged it out of the air. Fagan returned to the truck for the shotgun and headed for the house.

CHAPTER 37

DOWNSTAIRS, UPSTAIRS, IN MY LADY'S CHAMBER

Fagan circumnavigated the house. The front door faced west. One lit window in the back punctuated the otherwise featureless south-facing wall. There was a slanted storm cellar door to the east, probably used to deliver coal. The ground reared up thirty feet beyond revealing limestone gums. The fireplace backed up against the north wall. The exposed stone chimney was flanked on either side by mullioned windows and had an eerie facial quality. There was a term for people who saw faces everywhere. Maybe he had it.

The only light came from the first floor back. After circling the house Fagan crept up to the back door and peered in through the kitchen window. He saw the narrow hall leading to the front, the shut basement door. He returned to the front, entered through the open front door and inhaled deeply of what smelled like roast pork, steeling himself against what he might find. He went into the living room searching for the photograph. Doc had left it on the table. Fagan picked it up, experiencing a visceral revulsion at the sight of the uniformed

Nazi. No one had to teach him this—whether his birth parents were Jews or not didn't matter. He'd always felt it. Maybe it was part of the ancient lizard brain, an image of horror as natural as night terrors.

Maybe that's why the Nazis used it.

Maybe that's why he'd been obsessed with it. The nature of evil, one of the mysteries of life. Like a moth he circled and circled trying to understand without being consumed.

The figure was tall and lean with the silver piping of a colonel. Fagan turned the frame over and pried away the tin constraints. He slid the photograph out from between the glass and the backing board and turned it over. Written in old-fashioned script with a nib pen was, "***Standartenfueher** Heinrich R. Von Mulverstedt, Doctor of Medicine, Wahlberg Konzentrationslager, Gdaz, Poland, 1945.*"

Fagan looked from the photo in his hand to the photo on the mantle. Helmut Von Mulverstedt, kendo champion. There was an undeniable resemblance. The Nazi was probably Von Mulverstedt's grandfather. Why else would he have such a thing? How did people who came from evil live with that? As an orphan it was one of many mysteries he'd pondered in adjusting his attitude to his own fate.

Now that Fagan had a name he thought of Helmet Head as Von Mulverstedt. It made him seem less a force of nature and more a common criminal. But he was obviously no common criminal if, in fact, he had been cutting the heads off bikers for fifteen years. He was in fact a bizarrely successful serial killer.

Fagan stared at the head model with the leather mask. It bothered him. He placed his pistol on the mantle and carefully undid the Velcro straps affixing the mask to the head. Beneath lay a skull with leathery skin, a series of blue stars inked across the cheekbones, an inked blue tear at the corner of the left eye. The mummified head's eyes had been replaced with goat's glass eyes from a taxidermist mounted to stare in different directions. One of them stared at the cop. The pupils were gold and shaped like elongated hourglasses. The teeth thrust nightmarishly from the shrunken lips and cheeks. Maybe they could identify him from dental records.

Fagan inhaled and let it out slowly, extending his hearing

throughout the house. He heard the wind whistling through the trees, the creaking of the foundation as it continued to settle, the sudden report of a beam snapping in the defunct barn, the distant rumble of thunder.

There was a scrape from above. Fagan snatched up the pistol and moved silently to the base of the pyramidal stairs which had been shoehorned into a tight space and rose at a ridiculous fifty degrees with a rope banister. Gripping the shotgun in one hand, he shoved the pistol in his belt and grabbed the rope to pull himself up stepping next to the wall on the balls of his feet so as to minimize the noise. He rose silently. As his head cleared the top floor he saw a pair of red eyes regarding him from eight feet away and a foot above the worn and scratched wood.

The raccoon squeaked, scuttled around a corner and disappeared. Fagan slowly lowered the shotgun and his heart from his throat. Must have got in through the ceiling or something. He paused listening, letting his eyes accustom to the gloom. On his left were two doors, probably to bedrooms. At the end of the short corridor was the bathroom. On his right was the windowless wall. Pale rectangles indicated where pictures had once hung.

Macy could be in either room, incapacitated, unconscious. The silence disturbed him. That monster had to weigh two-fifty—his every step would signal throughout the house with creaks and groans. Fagan leaned forward from three steps down and peered through the half inch gap between the bottom of the door and the floor.

He saw faint gloom, furniture legs, dust bunnies. He laid the shotgun down below the top step. Pistol in right hand he reached for the doorknob, turned it silently and swung the door inward.

Nothing happened. Fagan waited. He slowly straightened and entered the room behind his nine. It was a den or a storeroom with institutional green file cabinets and stacks of cardboard boxes, many of them sealed. Some of the boxes were marked *Fassnacht Pharma*. Some were marked *Bayer, Neuer Aftrag, Rallopharm* or *Exodus*.

The room smelled of dust, patchouli oil and some faint

medicine.

To his left some kind of shrine. A ceramic Buddha on a hand-carved teak-wood table with inlaid mother-of-pearl, lit by a tiny purple spotlight affixed to the stand casting an eerie reflection on the walls and boxes. Three Nazi medals laid out on the teak stand: Order of the Knight's Cross of the Iron Cross, Order of the German Cross with eight points and swastika, and the Knight's Cross of War Merit with both swastika and Maltese cross.

The colonel's.

Below that a black lacquered rack containing a long sword and a short sword in their ceremonial binders. Before that a teak box on top of which sat a broad and deep ceramic bowl, marked with Japanese characters, half full of grayish water and a series of stone pumice blocks, one mounted in a wooden box at an angle. One of those odd Swedish "chairs" where you balance on your knees and buttocks was pushed to one side.

It was, Fagan realized, Helmet Head's polishing station. Here he worshiped his strange gods and sharpened his lethal blade. But if Helmet Head kept his sword with him, what were these?

Fagan rolled the seat into place and crouched before the shrine. There was a white scroll on the wall with Japanese calligraphy. Carefully, he reached for the long sword on the lower rungs. A *katana*, he thought. In Iraq there had been endless talk about knives, blades, who made the best, who fought the best. Everybody was an expert. Carefully, he drew forth the blade far enough to see the intricate scroll work, the polished steel. He could feel that it was old. It seemed to generate its own low wattage. He slid the blade back and replaced it in the rack.

A cheap garage sale desk hunkered between towers of files and boxes beneath a small window. A large leather ledger was open on the desk. Fagan flipped it open.

It was written in German and filled with mathematical and chemical equations, disturbing drawings of the human nervous system. Here, too, dozens of newspaper and magazine articles had been clipped and stuck to the file cabinets with magnets. These dealt with both animal and human cloning, stem cell research, the regeneration of organs in lab animals and humans. An old cover of *Wired* showing an improbably smooth androgynous person over the headline, IS THIS THE FUTURE OF HUMANITY?

The bile rose from Fagan's stomach as a wave of revulsion rose within him. He choked it down, leaned forward and brushed the heavy ledger aside. Beneath it was a black patent leather photo album, six by seven inches, embossed with the gold *Reichsführer* symbol and in gold script: *Gruppenführer Heinrich R. Von Mulverstedt.*

Fagan stared at it as if it were a venomous snake. He feared to touch it yet he knew he must. With trembling hand he unsnapped the clasp and opened it at random to two facing black and white pictures. He reeled back as if struck by a baseball bat. The black and white images were at once clinical and obscene. A naked androgynous subject strapped to a gurney, face contorted in agony as a serious-looking Von Mulverstedt in white lab coat and stethoscope prepared a syringe. Von Mulverstedt's hair was greased and combed straight back like that of some matinee idol. A tube connected to a clear plastic bag filled with dark liquid went into one of the subject's eyes.

The other was worse.

Fagan closed the album. He listened to the old house creak. The faintest rumble of thunder. The storm was moving off.

He pulled open the file drawer on his left. Hanging files in alphabetical order in German. Fagan found receipts for everything from medical supplies to canned peaches, all delivered to a private post office box in Paducah. Smart. Von Mulverstedt could visit at any hour of the day or night avoiding scrutiny.

Fagan found accounts in Germany and the Cayman Islands, receipts for a Gold Visa in the name of Helmut Von Mulverstedt.

Hiding in plain sight. A phantom. The First Bank of Cayman paid the utility and credit card bills electronically. Von Mulverstedt appeared to be tech savvy but there was no computer. Maybe somewhere else.

Fagan pushed himself away from the desk with a scrape and

went to the next room. Standing to one side he used his left hand to turn the knob and push the door inward. There was no response. Fagan stepped through pistol first and swept the room.

Heartbreak.

The monastic cot, the thrift store nightstand, the photo on the bureau. It was a color photo of a smiling, handsome man holding his beautiful wife, a dead ringer for Janet, wearing a red dress with the two smiling kids in front. It looked like it had been

taken somewhere in the country, perhaps after they'd embarked on their American journey in their rental car.

Helmut had been a good-looking dude, a Marlboro man, a rangy matinee idol, a German Eastwood. She was a stunner. They could have been Hollywood royalty or a Norman Rockwell painting.

The only wall decoration was a cheaply framed Doctorate of Microbiology from the *Medizinische Fakultut, Friedrich-Alexander*. It was badly torn and a little burned. The bed bore a slight indentation—not the monster's. The closet door stood open revealing the four grotesque leather suits and helmets.

Where'd he get the money?

Fagan opened the bureau drawer.

A Walther P38 lay in its well-oiled holster. Fagan picked it up, undid the clasp and withdrew it. There were swastikas on the grip. He replaced the pistol. There was a box of Wolf ammo and a dozen pair identical white gym socks.

He went through the other drawers. A dozen pair black short-sleeved cotton tees, size XXL. A dozen black jockey shorts.

Satisfied Macy wasn't on the second floor Fagan slung the shotgun over his shoulder and descended with his pistol in one hand. The roast pork aroma was tantalizing and sickening. Fagan circled through the living room and tiny dining area into the kitchen. The light over the stove was on, the black roasting pot shoved to the back.

He pulled the pot toward him. It was warm but not hot. He lifted the lid, slammed it back and shoved the pot to the back of the stove.

Some terrible Teutonic ritual. Von Mulverstedt was a scientist! Why would he eat the head?

Fagan listened. The stove clicked as it cooled. The house cracked as it settled. Thunder rumbled a long ways off. Fagan plucked the newspaper clipping off the counter and read with disbelief about the tragic ending to the Von Mulverstedt family vacation.

How could Fullerton not know this?!

Where did the paralyzed Von Mulverstedt recuperate? How did he regain use of his limbs? His story had earthshaking ramifications for the world of medicine. What if he had regenerated his entire nervous system? The monster in black leather was fast as a cat and strong as a horse.

Fagan instantly deduced that the Von Mulverstedts had been run off the road by bikers. What other possible motive was there? The man was consumed with hatred. His interest in Macy was obvious—she was a dead ringer for Von Mulverstedt's late wife.

Fagan scanned the news clippings looking for a name. Ingrid.

Von Mulverstedt loved his wife so perhaps Macy was not in immediate danger.

That left only one area unexplored.

CHAPTER 38
THE BASEMENT

The scarred wooden door opened with a creak. The basement steps were the same impossible slope as the others. The banister started at ground level and sloped down into stygian darkness. Fagan found a light switch at the head of the stairs and flicked it without result. He turned on his pen light and stuck it in his teeth, gripping the pistol in his left hand and the banister with his right.

Fagan inched down the steps straining for the slightest sound. With each descent sound seemed to retreat so that by the time he reached the bottom he might as well have been inside a cave. The basement smelled of damp, coal, ammonia and other chemicals. Putting the pen light in his hand, Fagan did a slow three-sixty. The wall directly before him in front of the house was rough concrete. A wooden work bench filled the narrow space. Pegboard on the wall held hammers, chisels, pliers, screwdrivers and other tools. There was a drill press and a compound miter saw fastened to the bench, and a vise.

A forty-eight ounce soup can stripped of its label and a small sauce pot rested on the counter. Plastic bins held circuitry, boards, transistors, capacitors. Everything was neatly organized, every piece in its place.

To its right a relatively new wall bisected the basement. It was finished in knotty pine and felt solid to Fagan's touch. There was a metal door set flush with a metal frame in the middle. Three steps cut out of the floor led down to the door. If Fagan hadn't shined a light on it he might have broken his neck. On Fagan's left were floor-to-ceiling metal warehouse shelves holding a dozen enormous jars.

They reminded him of his own basement bedroom.

For a second Fagan thought they might be specimens or pickled pigs heads. He shone the light directly on one. Bulging eyes stared sightlessly in an emaciated face. Quarter-sized black discs were affixed to the forehead with wires running up through the lid. There were gauges and circuit boards on the lid, wires running to a power source. It was difficult to tell the race or age of the head in the jar. Only the tats had not deteriorated in some way. Fagan could not stop himself from looking at the three other jars on the shelf. And then at the ones below. Feeling detached and under enormous pressure he returned his gaze to the nearest jar. A stream of bubbles escaped from the head. The massive yellow eyes swiveled and fixed on Fagan.

Help me, the head mouthed.

A leather clad arm snaked around Fagan's neck and constricted, lifting him off the ground. Black vacuum enveloped him.

He woke on the ground with his head enclosed in a tight chamber. Hands went up encountering a smooth plastic surface. The light was dim, as if from a distant star. He wore a full-face helmet with a heavily-tinted face shield. Fagan sat up and tried to lift the face shield. It wouldn't lift. It was super-glued to the frame. He felt for the clasp. There was no clasp. The tough nylon belt fed into some kind of slot from which there was no release. No light sneaked in around the neck opening. There was next to no light in the helmet.

Fagan had dropped his pistol and pen light. There was no point searching for them. He had to get the helmet off. Fagan crawled until he found the wall. Paneling. It was the wall dividing the basement. He stood and flailed about until his hand struck a small weight on a string. It disappeared and he waved his arm until it struck him again, waited patiently for its gyrations to stop, seized it and pulled. A dim bulb went on directly over his head. A sixty-watter screwed directly into a ceramic base screwed into the open wood-beam ceiling. The ceiling was so low Helmet Head would have to stoop.

It was difficult to see through the scratched and tinted shield. Fagan went to the workbench and grabbed the smallest chisel, inserting the edge between the face plate and the helmet. No matter how he tried he could not get a firm purchase with which to pry the shield away. He gradually became aware of a faint whine. At first he thought he was doing it himself but when he held his breath the whine persisted.

He went down the three steps. The steps were jumbo-sized, two inches deeper than normal. Fagan laid the helmet against the metal door. The whine issued from within sending an electric current of terror through his heart.

His scalp itched to the point of madness. He seized the helmet with both hands and worked it furiously over his head in an effort to relieve the itching.

He had to get the helmet off. It wasn't just the itching. It was claustrophobia, too. He'd never had a problem with it before, but here, head sealed in a box in a basement it felt crushing. He couldn't breathe.

Gasping, he returned to the workbench. He put both hands on the bench and steadied his breathing, trying to regain a measure of control. He seized the hack saw. He tried cutting upward from the helmet base to get to the strap but he couldn't get a decent purchase on the tough fiberglass without fixed support. It was like trying to pick up mercury.

That left the miter saw. In order to cut through the nylon strap he would have to bring the saw directly up beneath his jaw against his throat.

Why were there no other cutting tools? Why no tin snips, blades or keyhole saws? A thousand red ants chewed into his scalp to the point where he wanted to hurl himself against the concrete wall and smash the helmet off his head.

Fagan adjusted the blade, rotating the guard back and exposing the jagged edge. The miter saw was a vertical rotating disc. He flipped the toggle switch and the saw spun with an anxiety-inducing whine. Ever so slowly he lowered his chin over the spinning blade. The first hook caught the strap and yanked the helmet down against the blade. The helmet bounced back and up. It was like taking two to the head from Mike Tyson. Fagan caught his balance and returned. He had to keep the blade against the strap.

The Pit and the Pendulum.

Again, he lowered his chin atop the blade and this time, using his hands and his neck, he forced himself to endure the savage teeth as they ripped through the strap and hit his flesh sending him reeling back out of control smashing into the metal shelves.

Fagan fell to the ground and ripped the helmet off his head even as he heard the splank of breaking glass and felt the splash of acrid liquid against his cheek. With a grunt he hurled the helmet at the wall. It smacked and rolled making a dry hollow sound. He got to his knees and turned.

An emaciated hairless head gasped for breath in a pool of viscous liquid, mouth opening and closing like a grouper's, wires attached to its neck and forehead. Fagan followed the wires up to the shelf, to a series of cables that ran behind the shelf, running through modulators to a number of pressurized tanks set up at one end. Some of the tanks bore a red skull and crossbones.

There were eleven jars on the shelves. Each held a human head. Most were looking at him, agitated bubbles escaping the corners of their rictus-mouths.

Those eyes. Some were sunken, some bulbous, some milky white with enormous pupils. All looking at him, pleading, warning, raw hatred. Madness.

Shuddering, he worked his nails into his scalp like a man trying to escape being buried alive. He turned toward the workbench searching for a weapon.

He saw the fire ax beneath the bench.

CHAPTER 39
THE SOURCE

Blood seeped down Fagan's neck into his shirt. There were no mirrors in the basement and he dared not waste the time to go upstairs and look. By feel he determined it was not a serious cut. He used duct tape and tissue from a box to bind the wound leaving a silver band around his neck.

The faint whining from behind the metal door had stopped. It was as if the house was holding its breath, waiting for something to happen. He could almost feel its faint exhalation as something stirred the air. He got down on his knees on the bottom stoop and laid his head flat against the dust-covered concrete floor trying to peer through the quarter inch gap beneath the metal door. He saw light, linoleum, and stainless steel. He listened.

Not a sound issued from behind the door. He stood, hefting the ax in both hands. His side was a throbbing mass of pain. His introduction to the basement had been so intense he hadn't noticed but now it came roaring back. Fagan stared at the door handle. Not a knob. A handle. The door was too high-tech for its surroundings. It was fitted with a dead bolt lock. He wouldn't know if the door were locked until he tried it.

The minutest brush of moan issued from somewhere up above, so soft Fagan was not sure he heard it. He froze, white knuckles gripping the ax. The front stoop creaked as someone stepped on it. The visitor ponderously mounted the three stairs, each step eliciting squeals and groans from the sagging wood. The front door opened and shut.

The visitor paused inside the door.

And paused.

The seconds staggered by like a noon train in the middle of town. Fagan found himself breathing with a high keening sound and forced himself to inhale deeply. The minutes stretched on. What was he doing? The same thing as Fagan? Listening, extending his senses, trying to divine who was in the house?

But if it were Helmet Head, who had been operating the machinery behind the metal door? It could have been an automatic compressor. A refrigerator. Or any other electronically timed device.

The footsteps resumed with an odd clumping gait as if on uneven legs. The visitor marched straight back through the house, threw open the basement door and started down as if he owned the place. Fagan dashed beneath the stairs clutching his ax. The area beneath the stairs was crowded with metal tanks, regulators, and boxes filled with circuit boards, transformers and switches.

The visitor stood beneath the sixty watt bulb. A mesomorphic body wearing filthy blue jeans, a T-shirt. The visitor had no head. Instead it had a circuit board and a tiny camera that swiveled on a gimbal mount. It breathed through a tiny circular valve inserted into its larynx emitting an odd wheezing sound. The camera swiveled with a tiny whine until it fixed on Fagan. The shoulders slowly followed.

It was Fred. Fagan recognized the shirt. Fagan ran forward and brought the blunt end of the ax down on top of the camera and circuit board. There was a spark, a whiff of smoke, the smell of jet plane fuel. Fred took one step forward and collapsed.

Fagan bent to examine the device fixed to Fred's neck. Fagan knew little about electronics but even he could see this wasn't the usual circuit board. It had a homebuilt quality—using folded metallic gum wrapper and tiny gold earrings for connections. The transistors—or whatever they were—were nothing like he'd seen before with translucent segments.

Fagan searched Fred again from force of habit. Nothing new. He searched more thoroughly for his gun. Gone. All he had was the ax. He really had no choice. If Macy was behind that door he had to go through now.

Gripping the ax Fagan turned the handle and shoved the door back. Fluorescent light blinded him for a second and he instinctively pulled back and to the side.

Nothing happened.

Gripping the ax ferociously Fagan stepped through the door.

Into a gleaming underground laboratory that descended another four steps to tunnel under the earth toward the hills. The basement level had an institutional linoleum floor and acoustic tile ceiling with flush-fitted fluorescent housing. To his right a series of six foot vertical cabinets with convex doors lined the wall. And here, at last, were the computers: a laptop set up near the cabinets showing graph charts, a desk model at another station against the wall.

Where did they get power? Where did they get internet access? Fagan had seen no dish antennae or lines but that meant little. Von Mulverstedt could have run the lines through the forest to a dish. Just looking at the underground complex gave Fagan an eerie sensation. Look what one man could accomplish when he set his mind to it.

Von Mulverstedt may have found a way to restore damaged nerve tissue. He had solved the insurmountable problems of keeping detached human heads alive. He had found a way to animate dead bodies.

What could he not do? Von Mulverstedt had come closer than any human being to understanding the secret of life itself and what did he do with it? The desktop computer was connected to a radiator-looking hard-drive. Fat cables criss-crossed the floor held in place by gaffer's tape. They all converged in the wall next to a metal door the size of a broom closet. Fagan turned the latch and pulled it open.

Inside was a massive copper coil made of half-inch tubing,

about six feet high. It hummed faintly and Fagan could feel its heat. It took him a second to realize that the coil was wrapped around an axis, poking up about six inches to within an inch of the closet ceiling, which was fitted with a concave dish. Fagan couldn't clearly see the axis without removing the copper tubing and he wasn't about to touch anything. The protruding top came to a point. Fagan stood on his tiptoes and examined it as best he could.

It was some bronze-age implement, a spear or a javelin.

He got down on his knees and looked at the four inches that fell below the copper coils. A staff of wood so old it was almost petrified with some leather shards attached.

The Spear of Destiny. The Spear of Destiny was the power source.

The slam of a refrigerator door made him levitate. Gripping the ax he stood and turned as the first of the headless bikers emerged wearing a Nazi-party armband.

CHAPTER 40
CHOP CHOP

The corpse's skin had turned deep purple and had contracted but not decayed. The muscles bulged smoothly and ominously as the creature, surmounted by a weird little turret with a single camera eye aimed at him like a tank's gun, fixed on Fagan with a tiny hum. A brilliant red dot passed over his face. Laser sighting. The thing was unarmed but massive, preparing to bull rush Fagan into the wall. With a terrible whistling noise issuing from a valve in its throat it charged.

Fagan went down on one knee and swung the ax through the creature's left ankle. The ax was sharp and heavy. The blow severed the foot and the thing smacked turret first into the wall even as its hands snaked out and seized Fagan's pant leg. It was incredibly strong. It hooked one leg through the open closet door and began to pull Fagan inexorably to itself with hands like grappling hooks. The patch on its filthy denim vest said "Duckie."

Fagan shortened up on the ax and brought the blunt head down again and again on the turret until he had hammered it a half inch into the neck. The body shuddered once and went limp. Von Mulverstedt must have concealed most of the circuitry beneath the metal pot. Up close it looked like a small sauce pan into which he'd drilled a hole.

Using the ax like a cane Fagan got to his feet, side throbbing. He felt like Hiroshima after the bomb. Light headed. He stared at the closed cabinets across the room. There were dials and controls on each cabinet. Maybe there were locks. Maybe if he twisted the dials and controls whatever was behind the doors would die. Once and for all. Be still. He started across the room as two of the cabinets swung open and their occupants emerged, one with its camera housed in big soup can, the other in an old metal canteen fitted to the top of the spine like a cap.

Fagan snarled, hefted the ax and rushed forward. The dead bikers moved swiftly with surprising fluidity. Pain shrieking in every joint Fagan buried the ax blade first in the canteen, inflicting a huge dent and causing the reanimated corpse to drop. Fagan whirled clockwise in a huge three-sixty, catching the second corpse with the flat of the ax right on the tin can which popped loose and splanged into the wall. A circuit popped and the headless creature trembled and dropped.

The room smelled of decaying flesh, ozone and acetone.

Where was Macy?

Panting, Fagan went to a counter containing a stainless steel sink, drew water, leaned down and drank deeply. He leaned heavily on the counter waiting for his breath to return. There was a mirrored medicine cabinet over the sink. He opened it. Inside was a bottle of aspirin. Gratefully he washed down three. He looked at himself in the mirror. He looked like he'd gone five rounds with Junior Dos Santos.

He could only go deeper into the maze. It must have taken Von Mulverstedt years to excavate this installation, even with a backhoe and Caterpillar. Someone must have noticed the noise. Why had no one checked to see if he had the permits?

Once he got underground there would be no noise. Headless automatons to dig and to blast and to clear. To stand around throwing *sieg heils*. Midnight runs to his drop box to pick up the mail-order equipment. Years to figure it out and put it all together. The man was clearly a genius, perhaps one of the greatest geniuses who ever lived and it all seemed to happen after

the accident. Like it jarred something loose. Triumph and tragedy in one metal mash-up.

What a waste. All those miracles—immortality, reanimation, stem-cell research would not survive the night. And even if Helmet Head survived, and killed Fagan, there was no way Von Mulverstedt would ever be taken alive or cooperate with the authorities. He'd engineered his own little Ragnarok out here in the woods. He'd cut himself off from the human race and declared himself a new species.

Fagan wished he had a gun. Then he remembered the Walther. He listened. The basement was silent as a tomb. Gripping the ax he hustled as fast as he could out of the sub-basement, up the creaky stairs, around to the front, up the creaky stairs down the hall to Von Mulverstedt's room. He grabbed the Walther out of the top drawer, released the magazine. It was full. He slapped it back in and looked for a second magazine. He found a box of cartridges and dumped a dozen in his pocket.

His legs went out from under him on the way down to the first floor and he instinctively grabbed the rope banister saving himself from a nasty fall. He hobbled back down to the basement half-expecting the lab door to be sealed from within. Everything was as he had left it.

Where was Von Mulverstedt? For the first time Fagan entertained the terrifying possibility that the killer and Macy were elsewhere. But that made no sense! Hadn't Doc told him Von Mulverstedt brought Macy into the farmhouse?

He couldn't remember.

Fagan dropped the ax and ratcheted a cartridge into the chamber. The broom-like wooden handle felt odd in his hand like he was an actor in a play. Three steps down to the second steel door, the one leading under the hill. Standing with his back to the wall, Fagan turned the lever and swung the door inward. A rush of cool damp air flowed past.

He stepped through the door. The cave was lit by a series of utility lamps strung from metal hooks sunk into the cave wall, some suspended from stalactites. Fagan turned to his left and his blood froze.

CHAPTER 41
TRIUMPH OF THE WILL

A red, black and white Nazi rally pennant the size of a handball court hung from the smooth cave wall lit by several spots at the base. It momentarily stunned him like a smacked fly. Black box speakers hung from the wall at intervals. What lay before it was even more disturbing. A professional deck finished in polished oak, twenty feet on a side. On top of the deck two gurneys side-by-side, one containing the unmistakable red clad Macy, the other a black body bag. A stainless steel counter rose from one side and on it lay a cranial saw. Fagan had seen them in Afghanistan.

At the front of the deck facing the cave a podium bearing the official Nazi Party seal: an eagle gripping the swastika. All it lacked was der Führer himself. You didn't advance in modern German society by flaunting Nazism. The conversion must have occurred after the crash. Or perhaps Von Mulverstedt had believed it all his life and kept it hidden. Psychosis in full flower. Fagan knew well the temptation to give oneself over to evil. He had made his choice. And Von Mulverstedt had made his.

Sixty feet across the uneven floor, a coarse dark gray concrete half-tube, convex side up, approximately five feet high with a thick steel door and discolored metal piping snaking back toward the farmhouse, disappearing in a vent in the wall. A pile of ash lay on the ground beneath the hatch....

Macy was not moving.

He was going to operate here? In a cave? Was there anything he couldn't do? With what goal? His dead wife had lain in her grave for months, if not years. Was he reconstructing her from DNA, like the dinosaurs in *Jurassic Park*?

Fagan limped across the uneven and slippery cave floor and stepped up onto the deck. He went to Macy, who was strapped to the gurney via forehead, neck, arms, waist and legs. He felt her pulse. She was still alive, thank God. He slapped her gently.

"Macy! Wake up!"

She moaned and her eyes fluttered. Fagan looked for the buckle on the strap securing her head. It was hidden inside the gurney. The strap was made from the same tough nylon material as the helmet from which he'd cut himself loose. Fagan drew water from the tap in the stainless steel sink and dashed it in Macy's face. She opened her eyes and stared at him uncomprehending for an instant. Her gaze softened.

"Pete!"

Fagan put a finger to is lips and leaned in close. "Where is he?"

"I don't know," she whispered. "The last thing I remember him grabbing me in that house and pressing a cloth against my face....I think he knocked me out."

"Hold tight. I'll have you free in a second." He slapped his pockets. Where was his knife?! His eyes swept the stainless steel counter and stopped on the cranial saw. It was cordless. He jammed the Walther in his pants and picked up the saw. It said Guangzhou Mecan Trading Company/Made in China. The blade was a five-inch stainless steel disc with tiny sharp teeth, like a piranha.

He turned it on. It emitted a high-pitched whine like a six ounce mosquito. Maybe Von Mulverstedt was off meditating. Maybe he was riding around cutting off heads. Please God let him cut Macy loose and get out of there before the freak returned.

That's all he asked.

"Hold still," he said slowly bringing the spinning blade to bear on the strap below her neck. The blade zipped through like paper and the strap fell free. Fagan quickly applied the spinning saw to the arm and leg restraints. Macy moved cautiously, testing her arms and legs before trying to sit up.

She reached out and Fagan helped her to sit. She seemed a little wobbly. Fagan found a red plastic cup on the counter, filled it with water and handed it to her. She gulped it down gratefully. He refilled it. She drank half and set the glass on the gurney next to her.

"Think you can walk?" Fagan said.

She looked over his shoulder, pupils contracting to pin points. Her arm shot out knocking the cup of water to the floor. Fagan instinctively drew the pistol and turned. Von Mulverstedt stood at the bottom of the three concrete steps leading into the cave looking at them. For a second they stared at one another, frozen. Helmet Head walked deliberately toward them, right hand swooping up over his left shoulder and drawing the blade with a metallic *ching*.

"If I can lure him away from the door get out of here."

"Not without you!" Macy said, hugging him and surprising herself by her depth of emotion. Fagan reluctantly turned away.

Fagan settled into a shooter's crouch behind the podium resting his forearms on the polished oak. Fagan was a trained marksman. At this range he couldn't miss. He zeroed in on the faceplate and squeezed off three shots in a tight cluster.

Helmet Head belied the laws of physics and believability. As the shots rang out the blade flickered cutting a complicated pattern in the air, catching a bullet with each stroke. Fagan's aim had been perfect. None of the bullets hit their target. Helmet Head split and deflected all of them. The zing from the vibrating steel lasted longer than the gunshot echoes. The repercussions continued to echo down the cave all the way to the hell. Helmet Head was the devil and this was his domain.

Helmet Head paused, hands in front, palms facing forward. *Whaaaa—?*

Helmet Head advanced. He was ten feet from the deck when Fagan seized the steel gurney with the body bag, whirled it around and ran at the monster, shoving the gurney over the lip of the deck. The gurney smacked Helmet Head square in the gut and he staggered as it fell to the floor with a clang, spilling its grisly payload.

Helmet Head's wail was louder than a tornado siren. Fagan clapped his hands to his ears. Helmet Head dropped the sword and fell to his knees. He gathered the body bag to him with a disturbing rustle and cradled it, no bigger than a large rag doll. Fagan turned to Macy, held out his hand and helped her off the deck. She leaned into him and stumbled but she could stand. Like a three-legged race they staggered to the edge of the deck. Fagan stepped down first then turned to help Macy down. Her fingers sank into his shoulders like eagle talons.

"He's getting up...." she said with barely suppressed hysteria. Fagan looked around frantically for a place to hide her. There was no good place. He was the only thing standing between her and Helmet Head. He walked her back to the far end of the platform and pushed her down to the cool stone floor.

"Stay there!" he hissed looking for a weapon. He leaped on the deck and pulled out the stainless steel drawer from the counter as Helmet Head stepped up onto the deck holding the sword back in one hand for a killing blow. Fagan threw the stainless steel drawer at him sending scalpels and hemostats flying. The blade struck the drawer and cut through six inches. Helmet Head flicked the stainless steel drawer off his sword with a musical chime.

Fagan put his head down and charged. He'd been a Double AA collegiate wrestling champion and studied martial arts in the Army. He got inside the creature's swing and barreled forward shoving Helmet Head off the deck onto the cave floor where he landed hard on his back. Fagan landed with a knee on Von Mulverstedt's diaphragm and thought he heard a faint exhalation behind the opaque shield.

Fagan sprang up and lurched back. Helmet Head had dropped his sword. He seemed momentarily stunned. Fagan dove onto the wet stone floor, grabbed the sword and rolled. He got to his feet as the monster sat up.

Fagan brandished the sword. "YEAH, MOTHERFUCKER! HOW DO YOU LIKE ME NOW?"

CHAPTER 42
ESCAPE

Macy crouched behind the deck shaking. The cop and the monster squared off beneath the Nazi banner. It was like a bad acid trip. She tried to wake up but things kept going from bad to worse. How did she even know she was awake now?

She hurt too much for it to be a dream. The feel of the oak deck against her cheek was too real. She was too keyed up. She would never sleep again. Her volume dial was cranked out to eleven. She'd need vise grips to ever shut her eyes. She could not unsee the awful things she'd seen.

Here was this man whom she'd just met, and she'd let him fuck her!—fighting a creature from hell. Fagan didn't have to come after her. He could have waited for the all clear and reinforcements. He'd already risked his life time and again. Yet here he was risking his life on her behalf.

Wild Bill had beat down dozens of guys over the years for the crime of simply looking at Macy, or commenting on her to a buddy. But that was different. She was HIS woman. He was fighting to protect HIS dignity. Not much of a fight. Wild Bill weighed 260 lbs and was in the habit of bull-rushing his opponents and hammering them into the earth with his massive fists. He'd never even come close to losing a fight. He always struck first.

The antagonists circled one another. For the first time Helmet Head seemed cautious. He feared his own sword as if it had properties separate from his skill. Maybe it did. Maybe it was a magic sword. Macy was ready to believe. She believed the dead could walk, that headless corpses stole people and that this creature from hell, this thing from her darkest nightmares, was invincible. It was only a matter of time before he caught the cop and twisted off his head.

So Fagan had the blade so what. Bullets hadn't stopped Helmet Head. What made him think a lousy sword would?

Maybe it had magical properties.

An insane hiccough escaped the corner of her mouth like swamp gas and she feared she was losing it. They'd find her babbling among the rocks if she survived.

But here was this cop. All her life Macy had searched for men to take care of her, to protect and love her as her father had not. She was always disappointed, always. She feared she was one of those women doomed to make terrible choices in men. She was guilty of magical thinking.

But maybe this guy was the one. Maybe this was her last chance for a normal life. He was certainly her last chance at life. If he hadn't showed ... well she had no idea what the creature wanted. She had yet to absorb the reality of her surroundings. One moment she was in the creature's bedroom the next she woke up with Fagan shaking her in a cave with a Nazi banner.

She recalled that flash of recognition when she'd looked at the picture of the woman in a red dress. Even their hair was the same. But the thing had been stalking Little Egypt for years! It hadn't even known she'd existed, unless it had magical properties. Why wait until now to claim her as his own? Then she remembered the date and what Fred said. Beware the Solstice. And it was her fucking birthday. She hadn't told anyone. The only one who'd known was Wild Bill and he'd always forgotten it anyway.

The antagonists' dance of death took them further down the gallery away from the door. Now was her chance. Testing her legs she got to her feet. She could walk. She was young. She could run. The broom-handled Walther with the swastikas embossed on the handle lay on the deck in front of her. She picked it up. She'd fired guns before. Bill had pressed a .25 automatic on her that she'd left back in the trailer, and she'd fired all sorts of weapons with the boys at retreats, along with some of the other old ladies.

She couldn't just leave him. It wasn't in her DNA. But the thought of creeping up behind that monster, insinuating the barrel in the crack between jacket and pants—if there was one—and pulling the trigger made her knees go weak.

She had to think of the baby first. She was certain Fagan would want it that way. It didn't matter whose kid the baby was, the baby was innocent. The baby came first. The fiend's back was to the door and for the first time Macy took a real look at their surroundings. The underground gallery was the size of a firehouse and seemed to extend indefinitely, the tunnel only partially illuminated by the work lamps hanging from the wall. It could be a major tourist attraction, bring some much-needed bucks to this corner of the world!

Nazi Cave! The Most Horrible Monster in History!

Of course there would be added attractions like a two-headed snake in a jar and a bearded lady.

Now was her chance.

Wobbly, she tottered toward the door into the sub-basement. With each step she gained strength until by the time she was there she was running on her twenty-seven-year-old legs, sprinting like Catherine Ndereba, leaping up the stairs and dashing through the hideous brightness of the fluorescent-lit linoleum laboratory, into the actual basement which she'd never seen before. She glimpsed the mummified head out of the corner of her eye, nearly slipped on the slick concrete but caught herself and bolted up the stairs hanging onto the banister for dear life.

She paused in the kitchen weeping and wheezing, leaning on the counter. She saw the blue porcelain roast pan and instinctively knew not to look. She found her way down the hall, out the front door to the smoking embers of the barn and saw the truck.

"Macy!" Doc called from the yard in front of the burning barn. Why was he sitting there? Why didn't he get up?

Doc, who'd nursed her through the flu. Doc, who treated the bruises and contusions administered by Bill.

She looked to the truck again. That thing could emerge from the house at any second. She ran to the truck, opened the door and heaved herself into the driver's seat. The key was in the ignition.

"Macy!" Doc called again.

CHAPTER 43
HELMET HEAD SPEAKS

Fagan drew the creature deeper into the cavern in hopes Macy could get free. He watched her make her run for the door and when she disappeared into the lab his heart felt light.

An electric current ran up his arm from the sword. The grip was made of stingray hide with a blue opal in the center. He could feel the centuries singing through his blood along with the blood of countless others—those who'd wielded the blade and those whose blood it spilled. He swung the blade effortlessly in a complicated pattern he didn't know, as if the blade were alive and cutting its own path through the air.

He stepped atop a sandstone table so that he was eye height with the monster. "Von Mulverstedt!" he said in his best cop voice. "I know who you are! I know what happened to you. Haven't you killed enough?"

Von Mulverstedt stopped. He was a statue with his hands hanging loosely by his sides.

"Your grandfather was *Gruppenführer Heinrich R. Von Mulverstedt.* Am I right? That must have been terrible for you, growing up with the knowledge that your grandfather was a mass murderer. Was he on any wanted lists? Did he survive the war? It could not have been easy growing up in modern Germany with that kind of heritage.

"You were a good man, Herr Doktor! You did good work. Look at what you've accomplished here! Your gifts would be of great benefit to mankind. You were raised a Christian. Why turn your back on the light?"

The minutest shudder shook Von Mulverstedt. Fagan was not even certain he'd seen it in the flickering light. Was he getting through to him? How do you get through to someone who cuts off people's heads and keeps them in jars? Fagan didn't know why he spoke as he did. It surprised him as much as Von Mulverstedt. He figured it was the Rabbi speaking.

Helmet Head reached up and flipped his black visor up over the top of the helmet. His face remained in deep shadow but Fagan thought he saw a glimpse of a smile. He probably imagined it.

"You are za cop," Helmet Head in a high raspy voice.

"I'm a cop."

"She iss your woman?" Voman.

"I just met her."

Helmet Head lapsed into silence.

"What was your wife's name?" Fagan said.

"Gretchen. She was carrying our third child."

"I know. I'm sorry. Macy's pregnant. You know that, right? What's your plan? Put your dead wife's brain in Macy's body? How you gonna do that? Isn't her brain pretty much finished by now?"

Helmet Head reached up and flipped down the visor with a devastating click. He turned and strode toward the platform. Fagan felt a surge of voltage through his blood, leaped off the rock and ran silently after him sword upraised. Helmet Head broke into a run, gained the deck in an instant, reached beneath the podium and withdrew an ancient sword—far older than the katana, made of some strange flat gray metal.

Fagan had never trained in swordsmanship. But like all cops he had extensive training with the baton. On the deck Helmet Head towered over him. Fagan backed off, wary that HH could reach him in a single leap. Helmet Head moved like an Olympic athlete.

Gripping the bronze-age sword in both hands, Helmet Head jumped off the deck and ran at Fagan like a runaway locomotive. Fagan spun and dipped to one side aiming the sword at the monster's ankle but with superhuman reflexes Helmet Head saw the blow and leaped over it, bringing the heavy sword down on Fagan's head. Fagan dodged just in time taking the blow on his shoulder sending a shockwave of pain followed by numbness.

How had he ever thought he would survive this?

Fagan dropped the sword from lifeless fingers.

Helmet Head tossed aside the claymore. It landed with a dull clang. Helmet Head seized Fagan by the throat in one enormous hand and lifted him to eye level. Fagan hung gasping for breath ten inches from the inscrutable black face plate.

Fagan reached out and flipped up the lid.

Von Mulverstedt looked like a mangrove root. The human characteristics were there—the eyes, the nose, the mouth—but they seemed desiccated, transformed by alchemy into something fibrous and mummified. The eyes were deep-set, as cold and blue as the fjords. On the forehead creeping beneath the fiberglass a crude swastika tattoo. Like der Golem. As the world started to turn black Fagan thought how easy it would be to reach out and erase the sigil and the golem would fall to the earth as if its strings had been cut.

He thought he saw Macy turning toward them holding a stick and then he saw a long tunnel with a light at the end.

CHAPTER 44
TRUE LOVE TRIUMPHS

Doc had blown out his knee. Macy helped carry him to the truck where he boosted himself into the bed with his hands and lay down, cradling his knee.

"I've got to go back," Macy said.

"Do what you gotta," Doc grunted. He pulled his five shot from his vest and cradled it like a baby. They both knew it was worthless against Helmet Head. Doc was not going to be one of Helmet Head's trophies.

The outside air had snapped Macy into focus. She was ready to do what had to be done. She'd seen the shotgun on the kitchen table when she'd come out. She went back in the house, down the corridor to the gag-inducing kitchen and picked up the shotgun. It was a pump action Remington. Fred may have loaded it with deer slugs.

She descended the vertigo-inducing stairs hanging on to the banister, stepped over the shattered glass and body parts to go down to the first sub-basement. This time she looked at what she'd studiously ignored on the way out—the three headless biker corpses in grotesque sprawls with their tin can turrets smashed down into their necks. Her stomach flip-flopped. She sucked it up and went down the three broad concrete steps through the door into Nazi Central.

All Macy knew about the Nazis was they were bad. They were the world-standard in evil, apparently, since every time a politician wished to vilify his opponents he would call them Nazis or compare someone to Hitler. They were the bad guys in World War II. They hated the Jews.

That's all Macy knew. She'd never studied WW II. Hadn't been part of her high school curriculum. She never watched WW II movies. Those were part of another era. She never, ever thought about Nazis unless they were thrust upon her. Her father avoided the draft during Vietnam through sheer luck and a high lottery number. He never talked about it. It blew her mind that at one time the government actually forced young people into military service. Except for 9/11 she'd never known war, and that had barely touched her. The Muslims she met at nursing school all seemed to be nice people, if insular.

A boyfriend told her that all the Muslims were closet Nazis and wanted to exterminate the Jews. A girlfriend told her Islam was just another great religion and only sought to live in peace with its neighbors.

Now Nazis had been thrust upon her.

The temperature dropped fifteen degrees as she stepped through the door into the cave. Helmet Head stood with legs spread holding Fagan from his right hand as Fagan kicked and twitched. Macy leaped off the landing running barefoot across the cool, damp cave floor. Helmet Head was oblivious until she shoved the muzzle up under the lip of his leather jacket from behind and jerked the trigger.

The explosion made the leather jacket balloon outward. Smoke and hair puffed from the sleeves. Helmet Head staggered forward and dropped Fagan. Helmet Head limped away clutching his side. Macy knelt next to Fagan and took his head in her hands.

"Pete!" she cried.

Sightless eyes stared up.

All the air left her like a cockpit open to space. She feared she might disappear into herself like a black hole, sucked down to microscopic size. Nothing left. But there was fresh life inside her

and she couldn't speak for him. It wasn't her choice to lay down beside the cop and die. She had a baby to consider.

In her mind the baby was now Fagan's.

She had to get out. She looked up. Helmet Head sat on the edge of the deck holding his middle staring at the ground.

Die, you motherfucker!

Hanging onto the shotgun she stood and booked, taking the three concrete steps in a single leap. She'd run track in high school, medaled in several events. She flew through the hideously bright lab, up the basement steps out through the front door to the truck. Doc lay in back with a bottle of Four Roses he'd found beneath a pile of rags, feeling no pain.

"As we say goodbye to Happy Valley ..." he sang as Macy leaped into the driver's seat, set the shotgun next to her and turned the key. The truck started immediately. She gnashed it into gear and let out the clutch. The truck lurched forward spraying gravel and she concentrated on the wild bobbing of the headlights as she wrestled with the wheel down the rutted twisting path. The truck burst from the undergrowth onto the road beneath a clear sky. The storm had moved on.

The old engine bellowed as Macy pressed the gas pedal to the floor. She double-clutched the upshift as she'd often seen Fred do. Macy could handle a manual. By the time she crested the rise they were going 45 mph. Far off to the east she saw lightning flicker, had forgotten about it by the time the rumble reached her. The eastern horizon began to lighten. The truck plunged into the next gully. Doc started singing the Creedence Clearwater songbook beginning with "Down on the Corner," his drunken voice drifting in through the open windows along with the rich, humid air.

Macy turned the radio on and jumped in her seat. Her head would have hit the headliner if she hadn't been wearing the seatbelt.

"... utility crews have been working since midnight to restore power to rural Bullard and Lafayette Counties. Once again authorities caution you to avoid driving state highways 123, 38, and 55. Road crews are out now removing storm debris. To repeat, there has been extensive property damage and   reports   of

injuries, but no deaths have been reported so far. Stay tuned to this station for further information."

The farm report came on. Macy wept with relief. With any luck the power would be restored at the Kongo Klub. She worked on her story. She didn't want them to think she was crazy. She would simply tell them everybody but her and Doc were dead and the bodies were out at that old farm on Milton's Hollow.

Doc sang "Run Through the Jungle." Trees and limbs lay all over the road but somehow Macy navigated her way through going around when possible and over when not. The waking cry of birds filled the forest. Macy came to a fork in the road. She was unsure of the route back but knew that eventually both roads hooked up with highway 123 and the KK. The right fork descended into darkness and chaos. The left fork ascended by a fallow field. She took the left fork.

It was light out by the time she reached the highway. A SHP car streamed by lights flashing silently through the trees as she approached. Traffic was light—a few cars and trucks, but at least it was moving. Macy turned right and drove west nine miles to the Kongo Klub. The power pole was still down. She gave it a wide berth as she pulled up in front of the club and got out, glancing at the plywood sheet that covered the front window.

She stepped around to the bed. Doc was sprawled on his ass drunk as a bishop, slurring words and waving the empty bottle of Four Roses.

"Nice, Doc," she said. Praying that telephone service had been restored she opened the door and stepped into the darkened club.

CHAPTER 45
'ONE FOR THE ROAD

The generator had run out of gas but enough light crept in through the north window and front door to see. Macy went behind the bar and reached for the phone. She plunked it on the counter with a ding and picked up the receiver. Dead. But maybe her cell phone was working. It was still in her purse which remained beneath the bar. Next to the bottle of 110 proof corn liquor that Fred brought out for special occasions.

Well if this wasn't a special occasion what was. Macy reached for the brown earthenware jug, unstopped it and poured two inches into a cut glass tumbler. It was she who'd doodled the skull and crossbones on the side. The booze hit her like a blanket fresh out of the dryer. She felt the warmth spreading throughout her limbs, wished she could finish the whole jug, lie on her back and sing the Creedence Clearwater songbook like Doc. She slumped on the bar, exhausted. Christ what she'd give for a cig, but she'd already tried that and look what it got her.

She set her purse on the bar top. It was one of those backpack purses made of canvas with two leather straps. She fished around and found her phone, flipped it open and dialed 9-1-1.

"This is Bullard County Emergency Services. Due to a high level of activity we are unable to handle your call right now. Please leave a message and we will get back to you as soon as possible."

Macy could have screamed. When the voice told her how to leave a number or stay on the line for call-back options, she did scream in sheer anger and frustration. She had to will herself to calm down and speak coherently. Her voice was tight.

"This is Macy Hanson at the Kongo Klub on Highway 123. Fred is dead, Officer Fagan is dead. Most of the Road Dogs are dead. Get out here as soon as you can."

She thought maybe she should call her folks. Not that they were concerned. They really didn't care. They hadn't called her, probably were blissfully unaware of the severe weather. They'd sent a card on her last birthday, two weeks late.

The lights flickered and went on. The refrigerator behind the bar began to hum. The neon sign over the door flickered orange in the morning light—she could see the reflection in the glass.

Macy sat in an old folding lawn chair Fred kept behind the bar and patted her stomach. "We did it," she said. She was thirsty. She got up, opened the beer cooler and pulled a homogenized orange juice. Sighing, she sat, twisted off the cap and drained it in eleven steady gulps.

She would name the boy Fagan. She knew it was a boy in the same way she knew the smell of fresh-mown hay. It was in her blood. Whether young Fagan had a father was the farthest thing from her mind right now. After surviving the night she felt as if she could accomplish anything—finish nursing school, get a master's degree, raise Fagan into a fine young man all by herself.

Wait a minute. What was she thinking? Name the poor kid Fagan? She might as well hang a KICK ME sign around his neck. She laughed, breaking the silence and startling herself. She'd name him Pete. Little League. But no Pop Warner football, no concussions for Pete. And she wouldn't let him ride a motorcycle.

What was that song her grandfather used to play? "Soliloquy" from *Carousel*. Pete would study hard, get good grades. But he'd also be gregarious, a charmer, an extrovert who respected his elders and helped those younger. She wouldn't let him start dating until he was seventeen, make sure he treated women with respect. She would never let him turn out like Wild Bill never. She'd kill him first.

Her cell phone played Mellencamp's "Small Town." She stood and picked it up, too amped to remain sitting.

"Hello?"

"Ma'am, this is Bullard County Emergency Dispatch. Did you phone us?"

"Yes. I'm at the Kongo Klub out on 123. They're all dead. Please hurry."

"All right, ma'am, calm down. I'm dispatching officers to your location. What is your name?"

"Marcy Hanson."

"Are you alone?"

"Yes."

"You said Officer Fagan was among the dead."

"Yes! He sacrificed his life for me. He saved me."

"I understand. Where is Officer Fagan now?"

"At that freak's farm in Milton's Hollow! That's where they all are!"

Macy heard herself becoming hysterical.

"Calm down, ma'am. Do you know who killed Officer Fagan?"

"That fucking Nazi biker zombie freak! Helmet Head!"

"Excuse me?"

"Helmet Head! He rides around on a big black bike chopping off the heads of other bikers."

"Ma'am, currently we are experiencing extreme backlog due to the events of the past twelve hours. If you're not in immediate danger, it may be some time before we get someone out there. Are you in any immediate danger?"

The bell over the door tinkled. The door swung inward. Helmet Head had to stoop to enter the bar.

CHAPTER 46
CORN LIQUOR

Helmet Head is here," Macy said and set the phone on the bar. She backed against the back bar and heard the glass bottles clink. A rift split her heart into two lifeless husks. Looking down she saw her child's tiny bones past gyring vultures.

She bit her lip until it bled. Not yet. Not so long as she had breath in her body. Helmet Head was a man. Underneath it all he was still a man. She'd heard him speak. He'd had a family once, a wife that loved him and two smiling children. Another one on the way. A wife that looked like her.

She'd never had difficulty talking to men, getting their attention. Well this was it, Macy. This was your shot, your PhD dissertation, your Olympic event.

Stay alive.

Helmet Head stood inside the door motionless. Staring at her. She still wore the red dress he'd put on her, his dead wife's dress. That black face shield—like some kind of medical device—something that sent out rays.

Was that what it was all about? Looking for a replacement, or a fresh host in which to insert his dead wife's brain, spirit, zeitgeist? And how had he planned to do that with a brain that had lain in the earth for twenty years?

Yet look at what he'd accomplished.

Maybe he was some kind of Nazi warlock. Maybe he could raise the dead. If so, let him raise Fagan. Let him raise Curtis and Fred and Chainsaw and even Mad Dog. And shame on her for stopping there.

Helmet Head walked up to the bar. He seemed to be limping a little and his right boot left a bloody print on the floor. He stopped at the bar like some bizarre black communications tower. She could hear him breathing with a deep, rhythmic thrum that seemed to emanate from his very center.

Macy forced herself to stare into that black visor as if it were a camera.

"What'll it be," she said voice cracking.

Helmet Head raised one hand and pointed at the bottle of Jack behind her.

"Why don't you speak? I know you can talk. I heard you in the cave. Why did you take me? Do I remind you of your dead wife?"

Slowly Helmet Head used one finger to raise the visor. Macy gasped. His face looked like the Mohave Desert with two ice cold blue pools at the bottom of deep wells.

"Her name was Gretchen," Von Mulverstedt said in a thin reedy voice. "My name is Helmut Von Mulverstedt."

"What do you want with me?"

The blasted face regarded her silently. The finger again pointed to the Jack.

She reached for the earthenware jug. "You're from Germany, aren't you? You ever hear of moonshine? Corn liquor? That's something they don't have in Germany. It's kind of special. Would you like to try it?"

Helmet Head took the jug from her, uncorked it and held it to his flat pug nose. He set it down and nodded. Macy took one of the cut glass tumblers off the shelf and poured in a couple of fingers.

"Why don't you take your helmet off? You can't drink it like that."

Helmet Head stared at the glass on the countertop. He reached for his helmet, undid the buckle and lifted it off. Macy wished he hadn't. The right side of his skull was scraped to the skull, a white bone wall. The flesh just tapered off. Part of his right lips and gums were missing exposing vulpine canines.

Helmet Head brought the tumbler to his face and inhaled. He sipped and sipped again. He tossed it back and exhaled a rattle of satisfaction. He indicated that he wanted more.

Macy reached for her own tumbler. "Mind if I join you?"

Von Mulverstedt nodded. Macy poured Von Mulverstedt two more fingers, filled her own glass to the rim and poured it down Von Mulverstedt's neck. She grabbed a pack of Kongo Klub matches with the silhouette of a nude, lit the whole book and hurled it in Helmet Head's face. He stared at her dumbly for a second like a betrayed animal. The corn liquor ignited.

Macy took the jug and sloshed it all over Helmet Head who jerked spasmodically, flames erupting from inside his suit accompanied by little reports like circuits blowing. He began a St. Vitus dance, careening into the wall and furniture, trampling the broken stein shards and emitting an eerie high keening sound.

"Die you motherfucker," Macy said through clenched teeth and bolted out the back, through the storeroom, out into the back lot just as a sheriff's deputy pulled into the lot red and blue light bar flashing. Macy ran clockwise around the building to greet him.

The cop got out wearing a Smoky hat. He was young—younger than Fagan. She'd never seen him before. "You called about Officer Fagan?"

"He's in there," she said pointing to the club. "Helmet Head. He's burning"

"I'm sorry, ma'am, who's in the club?"

"The killer! The one I told you about."

The young cop opened his new Ford Taurus' rear door. "Would you like to have a seat while I go check out the club? I won't close the door. You just go on and have a seat."

The front door of the club exploded outward in flame as Helmet Head barreled out, head down, not looking where he was going, landing on the tarmac and running straight at them. The deputy strong-armed Macy around the corner of the car and pushed her down.

"Get down!" he yelled drawing his service automatic and swinging at the flaming juggernaut. Before he could shoot Helmet Head fell. His feet stopped moving followed by his legs, torso and arms sprawling toward them like a dropped load of cinders. His leather sleeves popped and ballooned releasing puffs of white smoke. The whole long corpse smoked like a Yule log momentarily obscuring the view. The wind whipped the smoke away.

"Jesus, Mary and Joseph," the young cop muttered crossing himself. His name tag said Ralph Underwood.

Von Mulverstedt was even more elongated in death, as if his ankles and wrists had telescoped. A smallish blackened skull with a few wires extruding lay atop the carbonized spine.

Gun drawn, the young deputy took his first tentative step toward the remains.

The tornado sirens went off.

CHAPTER 47
AFTER THE STORM

The deputy wheeled with a stricken expression. "Ma'am, does that building have a basement?"

"No. It's a slab."

The deputy looked around. "Ma'am, we're going to have to get in that ditch over there—it appears to be the lowest spot around. I think if we snug up to that drainage wall we'll be all right."

Macy looked up. The clouds were back, rearranging themselves like a giant lava lamp. It wasn't fair. Not after all she'd been through. They were supposed to skip the tornado. The air and wind had changed again, blowing sharp with a hint of cold. Myriad wind devils whipped off the tarmac and dust streamed across the parking lot in a river. The deputy took Marcy by the arm and more or less marched her down into the ravine that also served as a drainage ditch. A four-foot wall of bricks fronted the highway side.

They lay head to head at intersection of bricks and grass—the weather coming from the west—over the bricks. The sky turned bruise purple and for an instant the blowing stopped. In a second it was eerily silent save for the ululation of the tornado sirens going off all over the county. The wind paused. They held their breath. The deputy's lapel radio squawked. He ignored it. There was a shriek from hell and the sound of an approaching freight train.

All was chaos—howling wind, a whipping froth of moisture as if they were trapped in a clothes washer. Through slit eyes Macy saw a gray fog of meaningless motion. She shut her eyes and buried her face in her arms. White noise filled the sky.

Then it was past, eerily silent, the sirens stopped and the sun shining. Macy stayed where she was but turned and looked at the sky, then at the Kongo Klub.

The Kongo Klub was no more. All that remained was the concrete slab.

The deputy had her arm again. "Ma'am! Are you all right?"

Macy did an inventory. "I think so."

The deputy stood and looked. He took off his hat and slapped it against his thigh in frustration. "Shit."

His car was gone.

Helmet Head was gone.

Fred's truck sat at the edge of the cornfield one hundred yards from where it had been parked.

"What the fuck!" Doc boomed unseen from the bed. "I'm packin' my bags and moving to Seattle."

Five minutes later they heard the wail of sirens. The sheriff arrived followed by ambulance. The sheriff was a big man in a Stetson with a handlebar mustache. He went up to Deputy Underwood who hovered over Macy like a worried mother hen.

"Where's Fagan?" Fullerton said.

"He's out at the farm," Macy said. "I'll show you how to get there."

Fullerton led with Underwood in the shotgun seat and Macy in back followed by the ambulance. They had to pause several times to lift fallen tree limbs out of the way. The farm was no longer hard to find. The tornado and a possible downdraft had flattened the surrounding forest like a crop circle. The charred concrete base of the barn was all that remained. The house was gone, buried under piles of rubble: trees, rocks, bike parts, the Bobcat and topping it all off like a cherry on a sundae was Deputy Underwood's cruiser, red and blue lights flashing.

Underwood set out to scale the pile.

"Get down offa there, son!" Fullerton boomed. "We'll get a crane out here."

Of the Road Dogs or their tormentor there was no sign. If there were an extensive laboratory and cave system beneath the house, it would take a long time to sort out. Forensics would first have to go through the remains to determine what happened and preserve any evidence.

Macy knew they didn't believe her.

"Young lady," Fullerton said, "I think you need to go to the hospital. Vern!" he called to the ambulance driver.

Macy knew there was no use arguing with him. Any attempt to convince them that Helmet Head was real would only make her appear more unstable than she already must.

Then they found the cemetery.

ABOUT THE AUTHOR

Mike Baron is the co-creator of the comic books *Nexus* and *Badger*. He lives with his wife in Colorado.

Many people helped me with this book. First and foremost is Ian Fischer with whom I plotted. *Helmet Head* began life as a slasher film. Ian is the director of the by-now award-winning documentary *Rude Dude*, a documentary about my friend and co-creator of *Nexus*, Steve Rude. Fred Milverstedt, Tom Kinney and Stephan Hoff all read the manuscript. Fred was particularly helpful. Mean Pete Brandvold (www.peterbrandvold.com) was tireless in his support. Ellen Jo Baron and Tom (Doc) Delaney provided crucial assistance.